You Can't Talk This Way
and other short stories

You Can't Talk This Way
and other short stories

Danuta Borchardt

Baltimore, MD
2025

Textshop Editions is a collaborative project dedicated to producing limited series of experimental writing. It was founded by K. A. Wisniewski & Piotr Florczyk. More information may be found at: TextshopExperiments.org. Like other TE titles, the author has generously agreed to release an open-access version of this title following sales of the first printing.

Cataloging-in-Publication Data is available
at the Library of Congress

Library of Congress Control Number:
2025944798

First printing, September 2025

Book Design by K. A. Wisniewski
based on his *Smiling Lady* (2024).

ISBN-13: 978-1-7364658-3-7

Printed in the United States of America

TABLE OF CONTENTS

· · · · · · · · · ·

You Can't Talk This Way
and other short stories

Armchair

Long train journeys, railroad tracks going off into the distance, longing to ride on trains, wishing to visit deserts.

Riding on the train, like a gentle easing into the daily life, seasons going by with the arrival of the egrets on the marshes, mallard ducks swimming in pairs as a signal of a new beginning. And when the redwing or the night heron are seen no more, that is the ending of the year. Only the seagulls skulk there, with their nest-making and egg-laying between the railroad tracks, arrogant birds, more abundant in the spring, on the beachhead, where the rough and heaving surf tells the tale of the previous day's storm that does not subside overnight.

Neither the screech of the seagulls nor the plaintive song of the mourning dove sitting by the railroad track is heard on this side of the window of the train that has its own rumbling and wailing. *Trubu-bu-bum, bu-bu bu bum*, it says in rhythm with the graffiti (on the red brick wall) of copulation scrawled at night.

Survive this winter's storm, survive, but spew out onto the marshes from the innards of its home and suddenly come into view from the train, surprised by its own presence on the marshes, one stuffed, grey armchair.

Some godly hand must have put it there for us to marvel from the train; or perhaps for a duck hunter on the watch, or a tired worker, his shoes cast off, to rest in his travail, for a weary professor smoking his pipe—or for the ghost of them all

Perhaps a god or the devil, or someone's loving woman dressed all in blue, sits there waiting for the beginning, but we, the travelers, know that there is no end to the wish to ride by in the train, and to go on and on, and visit deserts in the end.

And while the trains pass by, a tuft of grass, taller than the rest, yet only a tuft, grows at the feet of the armchair and of those who sit in it, faithfully there till the time of the chair's disintegration.

Only the tuft knows the story of its final disappearance; some godly hand has put it there, some ungodly hand has taken it away; nothing to do but to ride on and visit deserts.

And so we went.

The Yellow Bird of Java

We were far away from Java when the shadow of the bird's flight visited us in Quartzsite—a small town and hardly even a town—in the Sonora Desert of Arizona. Why von Graf found himself there was a troubling matter and, for one whole evening and well into the night we faced with him his wish, and ours, for the immense and everlasting.

There was nothing unusual about our being there that winter which, sunny and warm as it usually is in that part of the country, surprised us with a subtle chill, especially at midday.

Quartzsite sits in the desert on a flat, arid plain like a humongous healing chancre fringed by an overgrowth of tissue, is surrounded by mountains in the distance. The town and its Main Street, an old country road, hang onto the highway by the thread of a ramp. We go there every winter, in January and February, when the plain outside Quartzsite becomes a showground for stone and mineral dealers. Usually, by the time we arrive, it would have already turned into a playground for stone and mineral dealers and their gals, and the Gem and Mineral Show would have begun. We walk among truckloads of quartz, jasper and agate in the rough, turquoise, chunks of obsidian, all of interest to Mert, my boyfriend, in his lapidary work, and also strings of beads to dress ten thousand necks, five-gallon hats and western shirts, biscuits with gravy for breakfast, if you please, hot dogs and chili at noon.

We mingle with the crowd and, like the gold and silver prospectors of the past we walk all day in the glare of the sun in search of the clearest of colors and most painterly designs in jasper and agate rocks in the rough. Moving on from chunks of rose and smoky quartz we by-pass figurines, bracelets and pendants chiseled in malachite, vases and urns carved in alabaster, yet linger by geodes two by three feet large split in two, and gaping with amethyst crystals from within.

In the center of town, thirst for a friendly beer has transformed a once modest Mexican cantina into the "Quartzsite Yachtclub." On this particular day, in a friendly spirit and to escape the glare of the sun in its semi-dark interior, we step inside. As our vision clears in the smoky haze, so does the meaning of 'yachtclub' two words?: one might think someone had sailed a ship through the desert and left his mementoes to decorate the shelves and walls of the tavern with models of schooners, old photos of sea captains, paintings of ships under full sail, and sundry nautical paraphernalia.

On this particular trip, as our vision adapted to the semi-darkness, we saw von Graf, a German geologist—a tall, muscular man, fair-haired and blue-eyed, the fine line of his lips a mark of his reserved temperament.

Now sitting at the bar, he also saw and recognized us, and pointed to a stool next to him.

After the usual 'hellos' and 'whatsups'—while we were settling next to him—"I hate the deserrt," he said grating his r's, "and the sun." To peruse rocks and minerals, labeled and priced, piled up and spread on tables in some God-forsaken desert was not, we knew, von Graf's reason for being here.

"Has Mimi arrived yet?" Mert asked.

"No."

"Where is she?"

"I don't know, she should have been here by now. I've been waiting several days alrready," he said, his hair somewhat disheveled, his eyes blurry from alcohol.

We had met von Graf in Los Angeles several years earlier when he was in his thirties, already a seasoned researcher in geology. He had done field work in Indonesia: Sumatra, Borneo, Celebes. And in Java—his yellow bird's territory, as we later learned. All along we had been intrigued by his choice of a vocation; but we didn't know until the evening we spent with him at Quartzsite how much von Graf's passion for geology was confluent with our own desires: to search for semi-precious stones as things everlasting. Yet, within the last couple of years von Graf's devotion to his work had taken second place to love, love for Mimi, a lively dealer in semi-precious stones, given to unexpected bursts of whimsy.

A few months earlier, in Los Angeles, we met with Mimi for lunch.

"I've just signed up for flying lessons," she told us.

"Oh?"

"Well, someday I might want to fly to those out-of-the-way places in the Arizona desert, so why not?"

"Sure. What else is up," I asked, half-expecting some other revelation.

"Nothing, really. Oh, and," turning to Mert, she said, "I'm sorry I'm late sending you the check, but I'll pay you for the turquoise and the agate by Friday. Come to think of it, Friday I'm cooking dinner at von Graf's? Would you like to join us?"

"Oh, that'll be fine..." Mert said, scanning our calendar in his head.

"Great! See you then."

On the night of the dinner, it was getting dark as we walked toward von Graf's house—we lived in the same neighborhood. Suddenly we heard a thunderclap, and it started pouring. We hurried on, then rang the bell. Von Graf opened the door. Something about him—the stoop of his shoulders perhaps—told us he was troubled. As we crossed the hallway Mimi stepped out of the kitchen. She looked lovely, wearing a yellow sand-washed silk robe and a Chanel perfume, I thought. She motioned us to the dining room. Apparently there were no pre-dinner drinks this evening. From one of her trips to mineral shows, perhaps Quartzsite, she had brought a piece of black obsidian the size of a large lemon for von Graf. This day she placed the smooth and shiny lump of volcanic glass in a bowl of water and surrounded it with fresh daisies and violets. It now graced the table as a centerpiece.

During the dinner the conversation went nowhere. Mimi

served us dessert. Stewed peaches in creamy vanilla sauce. I remember the sauce because, just as its aroma reached my desirous nostrils and the tip of my tongue touched its satiny delight, Mimi turned to me and said:

"I'm leaving von Graf. Not permanently, just briefly," she said, "but long enough to know how it feels in the gut."

She had to experience this, she said, to know how it felt in the gut, she said. She went on to tell us her plan—von Graf knew it of course.

"We won't see each other for a while... then we'll meet at Quartzsite; I've been there before, it's a rock-hound's paradise." As she prattled on, the vanilla sauce lost its flavor, and the coffee went stale in my mouth. That was how much and a million times more the idea must have pained von Graf. I remembered how he beamed each time he had told us about a date with her, about planning to ask her to marry him when the time was right.

"But Mimi, I thought that..." I tried to interrupt her. "I'm not talking about a mirage in the desert," she jumped back in, digressing from the more onerous matter of their separation, "it's a real place—you've been there," she said, "a fine place for von Graf and me to get together."

In the desert, I thought, where the air dries your skin to parchment, so unlike von Graf's preferred stomping grounds, the hot and green islands in the Indian Ocean, dripping with moisture.

We had grown accustomed to the side of Mimi that swayed in the push and pull of belated (though eventually, charmingly paid) obligations and, more often than not, promises kept. Yet, as I mulled it over, her plan to separate from von Graf and later to re-unite with him in the desert saddened and worried me.

That night I had a dream: I killed a bird, accidentally, an oriental bird. It was yellow, and yellow liquid gushed from an incision I had made in its groin. I had to pack the cut quickly or the bird would die. Finally the bleeding stopped, but the bird was dead. Or was it dead? I hoped it wasn't. I asked around, but no one seemed to know. If it were Mimi's dream, I thought when I awoke, annoyed with her and feeling sorry for von Graf, she'd be sure to kill the yellow-dripping bird. Just to find out "how it felt in the gut."

Yet I liked Mimi; she was a fine and gentle girl. When I shook hands with her the first time, we met the softness of her hands contrasted with the hardness of the stones she handled. I liked the way she would look at von Graf's piano: as she moved her head at various angles, its veneer of blond mahogany would reveal its chatoyance to her fascinated eyes that would catch the honey coloring and hold it for the entire day.

Mimi's flying lessons she had mentioned over the phone—although their regularity was subject to the prompting of her whims—were going well. She would soon be allowed to fly alone. But I worried that the unconformities and discontinuities of her behavior—just as these phenomena fascinated von Graf in geology—would, someday, fly in his face.

*   *   *

That evening then, in Quartzsite, before we joined von Graf at the bar, he had been biding his time by shooting pool. His turn was about to come up. Al and Mickey, our buddies from previous visits to the "Club" had already finished their turn. Von Graf excused himself, left the bar and joined them. We watched him make intricate shots, gracefully leaning against the edge of the table and stroking the cue behind his back. But he was losing the game.

"You Amerricans are a dishonest peepel—you make up the rrules as you go along," he said disgruntled. After a few whiskies chased with beer, von Graf was not in a gemütlich mood, and I thought we better let his remark go unchallenged. Finally defeated, he ordered another beer, and we moved to a table. He took out of his pockets all his loose coins, dimes and quarters mostly, and piled them in neat stacks on the table. We sat uneasily, not knowing what to say. Once in a while von Graf would get up to make a phone call and each time came back looking more bedraggled.

"Some peepel have seen her around back home… she must not have left yet. Others think she's on her way," he said after one of his trips to the phone.

Now in his forties yet straight-backed and still imposing, von Graf was, by any tastes and standards, handsome. And aristocratic—the 'von' would roll unassumingly off his tongue whenever he introduced himself—he could have reclined in leisure, though he chose not to, on an antique chaise longue of any Habsburg duchess.

We sat silently for a while.

"What shall we talk about, eh?" von Graf spoke up tauntingly.

"I don't know," I said. But of course I knew. I wanted to know how Mimi had prevailed, how she had managed to lead him out of the cool and scented shadows, out of the green and leafy shades, here into the desert sun. Mimi's lovelorn hate or hateful love that did not know itself was now failing to materialize during von Graf's long hours of waiting.

"What will you do if… I mean, if she doesn't show up?" Mert asked.

"I don't know."

"I mean… if she's decided…" but he checked himself.

"Oh no, I couldn't stand it alone back home, not for a while anyway," von Graf said, as if the possibility of Mimi leaving him for good had crossed his mind too. "Maybe I'll travel again—this time to Peru, or Argentina—for as long as the money lasts."

We watched his coins slowly disappear on calls that got him nowhere. Another mad Teuton, I thought, a Fitzcarraldo or an Aguirre, on a raft down the river of his insanity.

"… and make the natives cut through the jungle, make them climb mountains in search of El Dorado?" I said, following the train of thought of the Werner Herzog films I was sure von Graf had seen.

"Maybe."

Silently bent over the rough-hewn wooden table, beers in hand, looking into its amber to yellow, yellow to amber shimmer, we waited for Mimi. An empty cage, intended for canaries no doubt, stood at the far end of the bar counter beside a gallon-size jar of hard-boiled eggs in brine. In the dim light of the tavern I hadn't noticed the cage before. And on this side of the jar lay a few packages of beef jerky, while on a shelf behind the bartender, lemons in a small basket sat ready for the occasional call for whisky sour.

Suddenly, out of the blue, through linkages I could only surmise, von Graf seemed struck by an idea.

"Have I ever told you about my yellow bird of Java?" he asked.

"Your yellow bird of Java?" Mert asked.

"Yes."

"Well… yes… You mentioned something like that a while ago, never really talked about it."

"Let's get another beer and some beef jerky," he waved to the waitress, "I'll tell you about him."

In the dark wood-paneled, smoke-filled bar room (the only bright light shining over the green, felt-covered tabletop round which men, some angular-limbed, some pot-bellied, smooth-necked, or rough-necked, stood watching or shooting pool) we waited for von Graf to begin.

"Many years ago, when I was still a graduate student—quite a while before I met you—I went to Java," von Graf began. Focusing on the past, he seemed more relaxed now.

"This was to be a field study of local patterns of winds and rainfall. The monsoons had not brought enough rain for a few seasons, and arable land was shrinking. I had spent several weeks there, living on cassava and rice wine—prrosit," he raised his bottle, "prosit," we raised ours.

"—when I first sighted the yellow bird of Java."

Von Graf drew a long breath, waited for the oxygen mixed with the smoke from his cigarette to pass from the tiny alveoli of his lungs to the even tinier cells of his brain.

"I only glimpsed him at first," he said, "but with each trip into the field I could see him more clearly, till the silky, satin-like sheen of his yellow feathers became clearly visible.

"I kept my distance, and while the bird pecked at whatever he saw on the ground, I took measurements of the velocity of the winds and the dew point of the air. And so we co-existed."

Here von Graf stopped, fidgeted in his seat, then excused himself and went to make another phone call. When he returned his face looked stiffened, his mouth drawn tight.

"What happened?" I asked.

"Oh, nothing. Her folks said she's on her way… don't know why she's not here yet. As I was saying…" his gullet moved slowly up and down as he took a long drink of beer, "… so we co-existed.

"The yellow bird of Java lived where tall trees shade tea plantations from too much sun and from the yellow light of the moon as it rises over the mountains. The bird—the size of a goose, it seemed to me, but on long thin legs like a crane's or a heron's—walked about, slowly stepping over furrows. His shiny, long plumage reaching to his knees made him stand out against the dark-green foliage, and seemingly within anyone's reach.

"Anyone could see him, but he didn't care. His eyes were only for her, the other yellow bird of Java. I rarely saw them mate— only when the monsoons blew their strongest or the moon was at its yellowest."

Von Graf stopped again. Along with the clicking of the balls against each other and the rumble as they descended into the table pockets, I heard a drone in the tavern like a steady wind blowing on von Graf's distant island. Was he, I wondered, are we, bewitched, entrapped by yellow?—yellow as on road signs and highways divided by yellow lines, yellow as in traffic lights in transition from green to red? And in my mind's eye I too saw the yellow bird, exquisite in all his movements, stepping over furrows.

"He had no beginning and no end," von Graf went on, "only transformations: from egg to embryo to maturity. And before the egg there were two—one of each before conception—and long before that, the primordial cell. And even before that, there was before. Before the Cretaceous, before the oldest rocks became serpentines and mica schists. And long before the Archaean, and the Azoic, and ad infinitum before. You understand?"

"Yeees," I said, and, taking a deep breath, I felt transferred into geological time.

"But, just as important," von Graf continued, "is the forward in time.

"The bird's transformations would be of cells changing, changing, shedding plumes yet growing new ones as he was turning older, walking about, flying now and again in the face of time...

"He always kept his plumage clean and bright so that she, the other bird of Java, could see him whenever she wanted to, and especially when the monsoon was blowing or the moon was at its brightest.

"But wouldn't you know, his heart—as it turned out—was black."

No, I had not considered that possibility.

The game of pool was still going on, Mickey and Al taking their turns. Von Graf had not gone to make any phone calls for a while, an occasional raise of the bottle to his lips hardly disrupting the flow of his tale, his irritability all but gone.

"There was something else puzzling me about the bird..."

Good God, what else could there be? I wondered as I looked at his face—a sea of equanimity it seemed, equanimity which, while listening to him, I was beginning to feel.

"... he would never come out into the open sun. As he walked around or flew now and then he always kept within the shade of the trees in the plantation. Occasionally he ventured into the jungle that touched on the plantation at its far end. Not far into the jungle though, because it would be too hard for him to step over the underbrush and push vines out of the way with his long beak that was like a crane's or a heron's. And each time he came too close to the outskirts of the plantation and to the sunlit fields at the other end, he would spread his wings and take a huge, long leap right back into the shade, frightened..."

"Frightened?" I dared to interrupt, "how did you know he was frightened?"

"I don't know… perhaps I was the one who was frightened… by the shadow of his flight, perhaps…

"The other bird of Java seemed to call to him: come out of the branches of tea, come out of the vines and orchids, why do you always stay in the shade?"

There was still no sign of Mimi. Von Graf slipped into momentary self-absorption. In the noise of the tavern we heard again the blowing of the wind, while the old photographs and paintings of ships at sea bespoke of horizons far beyond the tavern.

"Did you know she'd be flying here?" von Graf asked out of the blue.

"No, I thought she'd be driving from Los Angeles," Mert replied.

"Last time I called I found she was flying here in a rented Cessna. Had she mentioned to you she might do that?"

"No. Well… months ago, when she first started taking lessons. But I had no idea…"

Von Graf cleared his throat and pulled himself up like a man who was used to self-discipline when addressing matters of his profession.

"As I was about to say—it was in Java, as I'm sure you know, that the evidence of the 'dawn man' was first found. Just before I went there, I came across an old account describing the find of his remains in Java, and now the image of the Java man with his flattened skull and heavy brow ridge appeared fresh in my mind's eye.

"The monsoon was blowing hard that day. I was more tired than usual, hungry, short of cassava and making up for it with rice wine. Sitting in one of the furrows, half dozing, I watched my yellow bird. Through the corner of my eye I could see the other yellow bird, not far off. She was calling her love. But the sound was like traveling through water and neither he, nor I, heard her clearly.

"Then, gradually, I saw the Java man emerging from the brush. He was coming closer, apish-looking, his hair sticking out of his flattened head and in black streaks surrounding his beastly face. I wasn't frightened for myself, I was afraid for the yellow bird, that he would tear at him. I lurched forward and grabbed the man to turn him around so he wouldn't see the bird. We fell to the ground and became tangled in leaves of tea and epiphytes whose petals, purple and green, stuck to my face. But in a moment the Java man was gone and there was nothing but emptiness around me.

"When I came to, must have been a while, the sun was at its zenith. I stood up. At first nothing seemed changed, but then I saw a yellow feather on the ground. I picked it up: it was soft and silky and gently scented. I saw a few drops of blood, then a few more. The tea plants were trampled where she must have been dragged by her feathers. In an instant, I dashed out of the shade and into the full sun. There were yellow featherrs everrywhere, and in their midst—shatterred pieces of black glass, shiny splinterrs everrywhere!"

Mickey and Al were still shooting pool. The falling balls sounded like glass breaking, only harsher, like distant machine-gun firing, but not as fast. Not enough noise, not enough noise to drown von Graf's voice as he was grating his r's.

"What happened?" I finally brought myself to ask.

"His heart was of black obsidian," von Graf said calmly, as if stating the most obvious geological fact.

"What!?"

"... when the yellow bird of Java saw what had just happened to her, the other yellow bird," von Graf went on slowly, thinking and re-thinking what he must have mulled over a million times before, "he leaped into the full sun. Microscopic globules of water trapped in his obsidian heart expanded in the heat of the sun, and exploded."

We sat in silence, stunned.

This seemed like the end of things...

And yet, and yet, going with the flow of his thinking, where, where was the forward in time he had promised us?

Von Graf picked up the thread:

"But the yellow bird of Java will go on. He has no end, only transformations. Yellow feathers baking in the sun, turning slowly into fossils, then into dust, into cosmic dust, and on and on..."

Soothed, I felt no need for reasons why, no need to ask whether or where do we ever end. He had just labored for the infinite, petals of green and purple stuck to his face.

Soon a country western fiddle would start its jumpy rhythm and the electric piano would begin playing. I had embraced von Graf's desire for the everlasting so completely, that these sounds did not have jar me in the least. I would have stayed on, this night and many nights more, were it not for the days intervening. But we had to leave and face the yellow sunlight of the oncoming day that would soon cast its glare. It was this—the inveterate incursion of daily life—that sooner or later we would have to endure, the yellow that confines us to our side of highways, that slows us down at traffic lights of cross-roads...

I was distressed by the bird's heart shattering, by the shadow of its flight which, sometime again, might cast a chill at midday. But von Graf's vision of the eternal came to my succor, and I felt grateful as we left the tavern, he and both of us, in our own directions.

By next day von Graf had not heard from Mimi, he told us at breakfast. As we were driving out of town a while later, we saw him walking down the road, knapsack on his back. Mert slowed down to offer him a ride but he motioned us to move on. The sun was hot, but not too hot, so far away from Java.

Our Rudolph

The big sister was like a huge rambling house, a mushroom, a fungus, a toad sitting above the three little ones. She was watching over them through her windows, winking at them with her lights. Her drooping breasts were like the sagging balconies of a genteel, old house. The three little sisters were perky enough, though low to the ground. They were looking up at her and she was looking down and, at first, there was nothing oppressive about it, nothing at all. But gradually, little by little and in barely perceptible smudges, grubs and grime encroached on their minds, the way fungus spreads and engulfs. Through leaves eaten by vermin, through gaps in the everlasting sky, mortification and horror seeped into the soul-marrow of the three little ones.

It all began at the one indelible moment when the crest of the bounding sky fell to the pit of eternal abyss. When the abbots and prelates, the great We, met their congregation as one meets meets another and lords over the little thou. When the big sister sat in the pew with her little sisters and held them by their not yet fully developed, puny wrists. The wrists squirmed and wriggled, but the vice tightened.

Outside the church the sun was shining. A breeze, now gentle, now brisk and rough, was sweeping leaves over the steps to the entrance. A man was about to enter the church when he was grabbed from behind, his arms held tight behind his back, and pushed into an incredibly beautiful car, white and shiny, golden trim all around. He was shoved into the back seat and driven off. The abbots and prelates were to catch up with the kidnappers later, such was the arrangement.

The man's name was Rudolph. He was to have joined his sisters in the church just at the moment when the abbots and prelates were to meet the congregations as one eye meets another.

24

However, he was delayed by a new and unexpected turn in the road, which took him through hollycobbles and hillycocks, pireas and putreas where the devilscums lived. Finally, when he arrived at the church, it was great, he thought, to have arrived there at all. He was to deliver his little sisters from their big sister and from the abbots and prelates. But the devilscums had signaled to each other in the field of the pireas, and the next rudolph that passed by was to be their victim.

The prelates had finished their sermon, the abbots had placed the last dot after We. All decked in their incredibly beautiful vestments, satin-white and embroidered in gold, they were about to leave the church. They were heading for the back door, better known as the vestry, when the three little sisters shouted:

"Where is our Rudolph?!" they shouted.

Their wrists half-worn through by their wiggling and squirming, they wanted to know where their Rudolph was. Their big sister, her breasts hanging like baboons on a sagging branch said oh shut up and behave, or I'll knock your blocks off. Their wrists worn thin, they were white with fear and wanted to know where their Rudolph was.

"Ah, la-di-da!" sang the abbots and prelates running out through the vestry, for they were in a hurry to join the devilscums, as had been arranged. They hopped into the equally beautiful golden-trimmed white cars and drove off with a whiz. Through hollycobbles and hillycocks and beyond the field of pireas they reached the wide-open country of putres and decayas, where the devilscums lived. There on the ground, stretched into a square like a painter's canvas, lay our Rudolph. They were serving Ginseng tea that he was hardly able to drink because his head was flat on the ground. They placed a piece of yummy bread in his hand that he was not able to eat because his arms were held stretched out. And so they tempted and teased him till he confessed: yes, those were his little sisters, yes, he was going to rescue them from the grip of their big sister, and yes, he was going to prevent them from coming eye to eye with those scoundrels—the abbots and prelates. And why, pray, was he going to do all that? Because, pray, he scoffed back at them, because he was going to save them from oppression and humiliation, from frustration, degradation and mortification, and from the la-di-da and from the I'll knock your blocks off in answer to their little questions. At which point the devilscums shoved a painter's stretcher down his throat and another up his ass, and that was the end of our Rudolph.

The big sister is like a huge house rambling above her three little sisters. She is watching over them through her windows, winking at them with her lights. All is genteel again, and there is nothing oppressive about it, nothing at all.

Manuela

Let us not doubt Adam's true nature. To all appearances he is a mild-mannered man, but as we watch him tend his garden we see him cut and trim a bush with the sharpness of a shark. With equal ferocity, yet deeply hidden within himself, he shies away from women. Though curious of each one he meets, he maintains a distance, because he knows that a woman will confound him every time, especially if he is thrown into her company by chance. Last night at dinner in his friends' home and this morning in his garden he is still puzzled by Manuela—a lively, buxom Hispanic beauty whom he had never met before. Today and last night intermingling, Adam is caught in one point of time as he hears in his mind the echo of her voice:

"I won't go to topless beaches ever again!"

He puts his shears aside. He feels too perturbed to trim his roses. Or to cut down with his machete a branch protruding from the old locust tree. He lies down on the grass, which is a thick turf of Kentucky Blue that gives him coolness and support.

The garden is Adam's love. As he looks at the flowers, a genital shape will once in a while intrude into his consciousness, and press upon his celibate life. A pink rose, the spiral of her petals coming to a point, will transform itself into the shape of a woman's breast, and join company with the pinkish-buff scrotum of a wild lady-slipper which has so gracefully snuck into his garden from the neighboring woods. And this morning the scent of jasmine halts his breath, and carries him back to the memories of his mother. Just then he realizes that this was the perfume that Manuela wore last night. A wave of tingling passes from his groins to the meat of his tongue. Adam closes his eyes...

They are all there, at the table, Manuela's friends and his, gently easing into after-dinner liqueurs and brandy. Manuela is sitting at the head of the table, her bosom well-placed over the edge, giving her a certain lead in the flow of conversation.

Manuela's ancestors were conquistadores, not a proud beginning in her estimation.

"But now my people don't spill blood!" he hears her announce proudly.

Adam's thoughts drift to Latin America. He is standing beside a man bleeding from wounds inflicted not with a machete in a lovers' brawl, but by bullets in the struggle for political power. No one knows which side fired the shots, and neither is innocent of spilling blood. He hears the sound of the Peruvian flute gathering onto itself the vast spaces of the Andes and blowing across the valleys, to live in the rarefied air of the mountains where there is nothing more for man to endure.

"I come from a large family," Manuela's voice assails Adam again, "and we'll have lots and lots of good little cilderen." True to her husband and to her Catholic tradition, Manuela extends this promise over the dinner table.

Her husband is sitting next to Adam.

"We are trying to make children, but no luck so far," he whispers into Adam's ear.

'Sometimes it takes more than two to have a child,' Adam remembers thinking to himself. Not for long, because Manuela takes the conversation to the pleasures of camping.

"I like camping, but I don't like changing clothes in public, not one bit," she announces rather loudly. But lest the company gathered around the table dwell too long on the prudish side of her nature, she shifts their attention to topless beaches, which she had frequented till the time of the burning of her nipples.

"I used to love those beaches," she says, "and one in particular. It had fine sand, almost black. In those days it was screened off by a wooden fence, but the knots had fallen out of the slats, and young boys from the neighborhood would peep through them."

Manuela's eyes are now like little globes oscillating in their ball-bearing sockets, intimating hidden pleasures. Adam remembers his ears growing bigger and bigger till they become the size of conches. They are also acquiring a hum, as conches do, till he no longer knows whether he is hearing correctly or superimposing a story of his own.

"I was lying in the sun one day, enjoying myself," Manuela goes on, "but that night my nipples were so badly burned! I won't go to topless beaches ever again!" she declares.

Adam's knowledge of the physiology of suntanning is limited, but he has always thought that there is enough melanin in nipples to prevent sunburn.

'Are her nipples albino?' he tries to imagine, not having seen them in person, 'or is it that they are particularly protrusive in the outward and upward direction?' he wonders. He feels his eyes becoming larger and larger and tinting with regret that he has not seen them in person.

"Anyway, I don't like dressing and undressing in front of others," Manuela goes on to affirm in full view of those around the table.

Adam opens his eyes and sits up in the grass. Across the lawn the silvery white 'Iceberg' rose does not tantalize him with contradictions, 'Betty Prior' desires nothing but to be trimmed, while 'Mirandy' talks to him in straightforward red.

'Roses are easier—nothing but to water them, cut them, eat them,' he stumbles over his thoughts.

He gets up to smell his choicest rose, 'Helen Traubel', and picks a few of her apricot-pink petals to have before his eggs for breakfast.

An Onion

Gray stockings were her favorite. They went well with all her dresses and set off their color to advantage. Red, blue, navy, coral, green. No matter which dress she wore, she knew all would be well, but especially well if the color of her dress was indigo. This carried her with gusto everywhere. But where was everywhere?

Everywhere was inner sanctum, everywhere was outer sanctum. It was the green underleaves of precaution, it was the overleaf of jeopardy. Everywhere was everytime, and everytime was everywhere. It would be in the heel of Amanda's stocking, once a hole appeared in it. Then the bald onion of her heel would take over and everywhere would be just that. The hole would take over the whole.

The onion was bitter and strong, and even policemen would cry at the sight of it. Especially one policeman, though he had even less than all the others the capacity to cry. But the sight of an onion in Amanda's gray stocking, in the inner and outer sanctum, under and over the leaf of everywhere, was more than he could bear. He relinquished the badge of valor that he had won upon approval, conditionally and reservedly, and followed her to the end of her tether. That was somewhere he had never been before. It was at the end of a green lane where preputias were blooming, and where the scent of heretofore was bitter and sweet and obviated the scent of the onion of Amanda's heel. Here joy rested with sadness and blended with the indigo blue of her dress.

Oy shoyle

Oy shoyle, oy shoyle, cried the little brothers and sisters. Their heads were spinning in one direction, then in the other. Their arms held on to each other in the manner of a link chain. They stretched from one hill to the next, and then to the next hill after that. When the sun went down you could not see them anymore but you knew they were there by the line of their song. Oy shoyle, oy shoyle, la.

They came into being at one end of the line and ceased to be at the other. Oy shoyle, la. Fatigue was carved on their little faces in the shape of wrinkles all turning down. It was more than fatigue, oy, shoyle la.

They had worn out their booties treading in one place and were now standing ankle-deep in dirt. Still grounded firmly they were waiting for messages from heaven, oy shoyle la.

It was night, twelve to eleven. The little brothers and sisters were spinning their heads while waiting for messages from heaven to fall on their finely tuned ears. The strain was more than fatigue. It was the tension of spinning and waiting, of listening and singing oy shoyle, la.

At five to eleven Orion stood overhead. He, too, had lost his booties, oy shoyle, la. Firmly grounded in space, he shone on the little brothers and sisters. Their heads stopped spinning for one astronomical moment while Orion, with his one spiral arm, tickled them under their chins.

All signs of fatigue, of more than fatigue, were gone for that one astronomical moment.

But when you looked at them the very next day you wouldn't know, for they were spinning again and singing again oy shoyle, oy shoyle, la-a.

Stuffing It

Malvina scratched her head. She walked up to the wide, double-door closet and stopped, unsure whether she should open it. If she did she ran the risk of knickknacks falling out of it. The last thing her sister Polenka had done before she left on her journey was to stuff things into the closet, heave the doors to and shut them tight. Malvina remembered her doing it: stuffing, heaving, closing the doors tight. There were antique dolls in faded silk crinolines, porcelain statuettes, fancy silver teaspoons, odd napkins from varied sets their mother had used during their growing-up years. Why her sister had kept it all Malvina couldn't figure out. She herself was always throwing things away, but then it occurred to her that it was like their social relationships: her sister accumulated, hoarded them, stuffed her life with them, while she, Malvina, was a hermit and didn't want anything spilling into her life—neither her sister's friends and sundry acquaintances, nor her knickknacks. She took a step back and scratched her head again.

It had been a puzzling day. First Ninzi, one of Polenka's friends, called to say that the leather holster her sister had ordered was ready to be picked up. Ninzi and her husband owned a boutique where they sold leather articles they made themselves, and Malvina had seen their work: belts, purses, etc., etc. But why her sister had ordered a holster Malvina could not understand. Anyway, she had already gone on her journey and the holster seemed to be irrelevant. But Malvina said she would pick it up that afternoon. Then Shawn, who ran a gun shop called: "Tell her I'm out of stock," he said, "but I'll get it to her as soon as I can." He would not say what it was. "She'll know," he said, and hung up. Malvina scratched her head and was about to leave the house when the phone rang again. "Malvina, your sister is a darling," Jodi's shrill voice penetrated the receiver and Malvina's eardrum, "why don't the two of you come for supper tonight." "But…" "I don't want to hear another thing, see you tonight." Bang. Malvina finally left the house to do her errands, and when she returned the house painters had already set up their ladders and were scraping the old paint off the house. They were a cheerful crew, gabbing, whistling tunes, scraping away, not wasting a minute. "Hey, Macky!" Malvina heard them greet their boss when he arrived, "how was your weekend?" "Smooth, very smooth!" The house hardly needed painting, it had been done merely a couple of years earlier, but her sister thought too much paint was peeling off. So Malvina scra…, no, this time she didn't (the skin on her scalp was getting sore), she just went along with it. And now the painters were there, all around the house, scraping, shouting, crowding her in. Yet—'what was the point of the house being freshly painted?' Malvina thought to herself, 'when my sister…' She scratched her head.

There was much to be done that day, but Malvina felt disconnected from it all. A few more phone calls and she would have totally fallen apart. The painters calling to each other, the scratching, almost gouging, of the wooden shingles grated on her nerves, she found it difficult to put one thought in front of another. 'When all else fails, take a nap,' she remembered the adage. When she woke up the day had faded, the painters were gone. There was still the closet to face but she put it off to another time.

A few days passed. The painters shouting, whistling, scraping, Malvina scratching her head. Once in a while there was a trace of blood under her nail. She hardly noticed the pain in her scalp. It was not until sometime later, when she was trying to untangle a clump of matted hair on the side of her head, that Malvina realized there was a lot of congealed blood in it. She thought she better see her doctor. He found an open wound that reached all the way to the surface of the skull. He packed and dressed the wound. Then, after much persuasion, Malvina let him whisk her off to a sanatorium where her nerves could recover.

*   *   *

Polenka felt that hers had been a dumbbell of a profession. Cleaning consciences, mopping up tears, wiping off guilt. She might as well have been a house cleaner. Her sister Malvina did nothing but scratch her head and got by. At first there was compassion but as the years went on, how could Polenka sustain compassion for states of mind that were increasingly being dubbed as 'chemical imbalance'? Her calling had been as a physician for the mind, not for the brain. So now she felt like riding off into the sunset. 'All I need is a holster and a gun to put in it,' she thought, 'I'll also have the house painted so Malvina isn't left with the old paint peeling off.'

She had a wide array of patients in town: drug dealers, gun runners, ammunition traders, pimps, prostitutes. Malvina often picked up cryptic messages for her sister on the phone, but didn't even bother to question them, just scratched her head. 'Some day she'll be in trouble with that scratching,' Polenka thought but couldn't do much about it. She left this mopping up to another physician, whose profession was to patch up wounds and have Malvina's nerves soothed with salves, herbs and send-offs to sanatoria.

Among the prostitutes Jodi was Polenka's favorite. She always had to get Jodi out of one scrape or another, send her to other specialists who would treat her vaginal discharge or vaccinate her against some exotic disease sailors were bringing into town. Once in a while Jodi would call her on the spur of the moment and, with that shrill voice of hers, invite her and Malvina for supper— no ifs, buts, or rain checks about it. There seemed to be little chemical imbalance about Jodi except for the meals she served: pigs' feet, gizzards, tripe, stuffed sheep stomachs—whatever men brought her to cook, she was their cook too—and well soused in wine. Now Ninzi and her husband were another kettle of fish— no pimping or dealing here—they ran a tight and clean leather-goods operation. When it came to having a holster made there was no one like them.

. If she had ever dumped her profession to embrace another she would have been a great house cleaner, without responsibility for anyone's psyche. But she hated house cleaning so she left it to Malvina. The only problem was that Malvina threw everything away, while she liked to hoard everything, including objects their mother had left. She stuffed it all into a closet, hoping that Malvina would never get around to cleaning it.

Time came for her to ride off into the sunset. The last thing she did (other than ordering a holster, a gun and a round of ammunition which she wouldn't pick up because she didn't need them, and the painters to paint the house) was to stuff the closet with even more stuff, heave the doors to and close them tight.

The sunset was that particular evening, the most spectacular she had ever seen. In pink and orange and green and blood-red juicy colors, and shimmering like the jelly around pomegranate seeds. It took her mind off her profession entirely.

She had done enough: she had wiped tears and guilt, scraped many consciences clean, she even ordered and bought their goods (which she never used, but which further cluttered her living space) so they would feel better about their professions. But she had had enough, enough of people and stuff, enough of tripe and pigs' feet soused in wine. But she knew that at the end of her journey, when the time came and push came to shove, all the drug dealers and gun runners, all the pimps and prostitutes whose tears she had wiped would do her bidding.

The sunset did not last very long. Night followed and both she and her horse were hungry. The horse came first of course, as any rider knows. He needed oats and water. Water was easy, but oats? Being a woman, she had never sown any, nor did she know how to reap. But she led the horse to a pasture, she led him to water to drink. He did. She then lay down on the grass to sleep, while the horse slept standing, as horses are wont to do. Next day and the day after, and many days thereafter they rode.

A month had passed and Polenka felt the pearly gates were not too far off. She and the horse had reached the high desert where washes retro-promise water in torrents of the spring just passed. She didn't know how many times a day a horse should eat or drink, but she fed and watered him whenever he nudged her and whenever she could. But now she could no longer. She let him loose. In the meantime, her own stomach had slowly shrank, her hunger abated till it was gone entirely.

A horse, seemingly wild, was roaming the desert. Following its tracks they found, under a sage bush, a desiccated body with a note pinned to it: NO BURIAL, YOU PIMPS AND PROSTITUTES AND RUNNERS OF ALL SORTS, JUST STUFF ME IN MY CLOSET.

*   *   *

When Malvina eventually returned home from the sanatorium she headed straight for the closet. She opened the doors wide. Her sister's skeleton fell out and lay at her feet.

Peonies

There were peonies everywhere. If that's where your imagination leads you, that's where the peonies were, in a small village on a cinder cone on the Arizona desert. Pink flowers, large like breasts of women who eat too much. During this festival venders were selling them in the streets, people showed them off on their window sills, girls wore them as posies, men in their buttonholes.

People were running to the top of the cinder cone, to admire the flowers from high up. Not so Melinda. She was running in the opposite direction to everyone else.

She heard someone running behind her. Reginald finally caught up with her and gripped her by the arm.

"Stop, where are you going?" he shouted.

"To the school, to my class and fetch the kids, just let me go!"

"But why, where are you taking them?"

"Down to the valley below, as far and fast as we can get there."

"But why?"

"Haven't you seen the goats, instead of grazing in their enclosures they jumped over the fences and run down to the valley, the horses stood rampant on their haunches and neighed to high heaven, cats dug their claws into dirt as if they were prairie dogs?"

"No, I didn't, you must have been imagining it."

"Just let go of my arm and come with me!"

He wouldn't.

A cinder cone is not like a Mount Etna, or a Kilauea volcano where lava and gases move around, bubbling, hissing, and give you fair warning. Instead pyroclastic mix of lava blocks, ash and gases burst through uncemented cinders of a central vent to the top without warning, then spread down forming a cone.

Melinda and her screaming kids were fighting back, wanting

to see the peonies, fed up with all the digital stuff she was usually teaching them in class. And now she was dragging them away from all the fun up the cone. But regardless, they were now far below, down the valley.

So far nothing happened. People were not caught in any eruption and did not see the pyroclastic mix, and Melinda, exhausted, was dragging her tired and whining kids back up the mountain.

"Where were our kids?!" The scared and furious parents were screaming. Furious for causing them so much anxiety for nothing.

And no, she would not have to dig through ashes to recover her Reginald. Instead, she was taken to a psychiatric center to recover from her mental turmoil and exhaustion. Exhaustion from all the 'apps' and the 'podcasts' and the 'iPhones,' she had been teaching her class. And 'streaming,' the only word she could understand was 'streaming,' and even that did not mean what it usually means. What perturbed her most was the comfort with which adults were uttering these words, like it was their daily bread, their bread and butter, the bacon they brought to the table, simple as pie.

By the time she was leaving the center, supported by her Reginald, her anxiety was gone. He led her tenderly to his apartment for supper he had prepared.

"The only thing I regret is," she said "that I missed most of the peonies show."

"Don't worry," he said, "we'll watch it on Netflix at my place because your TV is not set up for that."

"Watch it on what?"

"You know what Netflix is."

"Well yes, of course I do."

In the meantime, people had cleared up the mess, the wilted peonies, their petals trampled by the exiting spectators.

After leaving Reginald's place next day, while she was slowly walking home, she realized that something strange was happening. People were not sending her their smiles or their usual greetings of how are you, have a good day, perhaps blaming her even for the trampled peonies; the parents of the kids she had led down to the valley were especially annoyed. She felt she had done well by their children, she was a good woman, even animals liked her, her cat would lick her hands, sleep with her, snuggling himself into the curves of her body. But now she felt like an outcast.

Melinda didn't know how far down the pyroclastic mix would flow when an eruption happened. She figured a few thousand feet. To have at least the school kids on her side, she promised them field trips, one day a week, when they would go down the cone and place stakes around it to show how far down it might be safe to build houses. She showed them how to bang down the iron stakes with their little mallets, and they were happy. She placed them a couple of feet apart so that they wouldn't run into each other. It took them many weeks to surround the cinder cone with stakes. They were proud when it was done.

Sometime later it happened.

A few people survived, perhaps a dozen in all, and only those who happened to find themselves the farthest down at the time of the eruption and closest to the stakes. First on their haunches, they slowly cleared themselves from the ashes and brushed themselves off. Their faces still gray from fear and contorted with pain from the burns. One by one, they straightened themselves and looked about.

Melinda had been anxiously surveying the cone a few weeks earlier. As was her luck, she had survived the eruption; she now rushed to help the afflicted people as best she could.

One of the saved men looking about pointed her in the direction where her Reginald might be. She thought she finally located his foot but the shoe on it didn't look familiar. She fell to her knees, praying and hoping that her next boyfriend would wear shoes that she could easily recognize.

Humming of the Desert

He was on his way to Death Valley, deep in the Mojave Desert, traveling from Los Angeles. No angels there now, but some may have landed there before man. The first man to land there may have seen angels, or wished he had, to guide him though the desert.

'I want no visions of Gila monsters crossing my path,' was one of Walter's thoughts, 'not on my trip through the desert!'

"What does a man need?" he had asked around before he left. A few ideas of how things are: that spring is the best time to go, that it is too hot in the summer, that some come back and others don't. And beyond that—travel light. A flask of water, not much more.

His wife Annie had been to the desert before they married, she knew it as a place to dream about, to conjure up images and transpose them to her canvas. Like Georgia O'Keeffe. She had hoped that someday they'd go there together.

"Go to the desert, go somewhere, loosen up," she told him when they were splitting up.

"Nah," he said, "too much uncertainty, mirages of water. I like my water real, straight from the tap."

"Well, just the same I think you should go. See the canyons I once told you about." Those were her parting words.

Somewhere past Bakersfield, Walter stopped at a roadside Casa Burrito for a cup of coffee. Sipping his coffee, as he now cupped the mug in his hands, was one of those quiet moments when he missed Annie the most. Annie gone, and their young son Mark in the army, he had spent the past couple of years alone.

He wanted sugar in his coffee—unusual for him, he seldom used it. There was none on his table, so he walked over to the neighboring booth. A woman was sitting there.

"Sure, take it," she said, pushing a jar of sugar in his direction. The movement of her hand was light, a few silver bangles jingled softly on her arm.

"Are you alone?" he asked.

"Yes."

"May I join you?"

"Yes." He brought his coffee and sat across the table from her.

"I'm on my way to the desert," Walter said, "have you ever been there?"

"Yes, many times."

He waited.

"You're a woman of few words," he finally remarked.

"It takes me a while. I prefer to listen, then I hear better."

"You mean, you're a bit deaf?"

"No, I mean I hear better what people are really saying."

"Interesting. My wife used to say the same thing."

"Used to?"

"We don't see each other anymore."

"I'm sorry."

"Sweetening the coffee helps."

"I know. But all the sugar in the world is sometimes not enough. There was plenty of it where I had once been, but it didn't help."

"Oh? Where was that?"

"In Guatemala."

"Really? I'm not one for traveling, even to places close by, like the desert here, almost in LA's backyard."

"I travel a lot, I travel light," she said as she adjusted the gauze shawl over her young shoulders, seemingly her only upper-body apparel.

"Where are you going now?" he asked.

"I'm on my way back to Bakersfield, nothing pressing though."

"Would you… would you consider coming to the desert with me first? I'd appreciate your expertise."

"Not an easy place to visit. Why do you want to go there anyway?"

"To begin going somewhere, to loosen up."

"I see."

She looked at his square jaw, muscles twitching, but his eyes seemed gentle, some white hair softening the dark-brown of his beard. It was happening again—a man asking her to accompany him. The last time had ended in disaster. Her quiet wails, she thought, may still be trailing over the Guatemalan highlands. Perhaps this time it would turn out better.

She had wandered over the semi-desert many times and knew it well:

"Well… would you?"

"All right," she said, "I've wandered over this semi-desert many times and know it well."

"Semi-desert, did you say?"

"Yes, this is what this one here is."

"What do you mean—semi-desert?"

"It's one with some rainfall and vegetation, unlike something like the Sahara."

"Funny, I never knew that. I'm a stickler for details yet this one escaped me. Yet there is such a thing as common usage."

"Of course."

She also knew the smell of creosote bush after an occasionally downpour, the rustling of dry blades of grass, antelopes in the distance. She knew what thirst was, she'd heard a snake's rattle and knew how to avoid its strike.

They stepped outside the Casa and got into his car.

"Let's go first through Antelope Hills then Antelope Acres," she suggested.

'Enticing names,' he thought. But the winding, uphill road took them between shacks and car-engine dumps. No antelopes here. Finally they came to open country where the road took them to hills from which they could look over the Mojave: an expanse of brush and sands in the distance, and closer up massive boulders that impede the easy passage of the antelope and give shelter to the snake.

They spoke little, but before going on they agreed on a leisurely soak in a hot spring on the outskirts of the desert. Refreshed and pleased they moved on.

"I just saw some antelopes," she said.

"I didn't, I wasn't looking," he said.

They continued traveling an empty road across the Badlands. The rising temperature of the air promised the deadly heat of the summer to come.

"At the turn of the century they took borax out of here in wagons pulled by teams of donkeys," Walt said, "I know that much, and that people died crossing the valley to reach the mountains beyond." He liked reading up on facts.

A flask of water at his belt, an apple each in hand they left the car and went on foot toward the canyons looming in the distance. She stopped for a moment.

"I hear the desert humming," she said.

"It's just your imagination."

"No it's not."

Long before man came here, rivers tumbled rocks from the mountains on either side of the valley and left them at the mouth of the canyons in wide alluvial fans. It was the rush of the rivers long gone, the braying of the donkeys, the silence of the dead that she was hearing.

They reached one of the canyons. Its walls stood tall, cut and smoothed by torrents of water in times gone by.

"Let's walk up," she suggested.

A slow step at a time, a munch on their apples, they went between the canyon walls, stepping over rocky rubble and prickly grasses, and up the dry river bed. After a while they turned around to look at the sandy dunes covering part of the desert below, at the jagged mountain range cutting the horizon. The vastness of the land ahead, the smoothness of the canyon walls, the few white, solitary clouds moving 'like angels,' he thought, slowly, across the clear-blue sky made him uneasy.

"Let's go back to the car," he said.

"So soon? That's quite a sudden turn," she said.

"Yes… please."

Their descent was slow, the air still hot, the jabbing of the bushes at their legs no less persistent, the apples gone. They were part of the way down the mountain, as he was kicking this pebble and that with his heavy boots, sending the stones rolling towards the valley. Her feet barely touched the ground.

Suddenly he exclaimed: "Look!"

A few feet to the side lay a wooden object about a foot square and a few inches high. They came closer to it. It was a dusty, weathered box set on a flat spot of ground. They stepped closer and, leaning over it, they cautiously looked through a pane of glass on one of its sides. Inside was a needle pivoted horizontally toward a roll of printed paper.

"This is a seismograph," he said, "but who and why someone would have put it here, had there been earthquakes that needed measuring?" he wondered aloud.

"I don't know," she said.

'It must be here for a purpose,' she thought, 'don't touch!' flashed through her mind, 'don't touch embers!' came a voice from her recent past.

They walked around the box, puzzled. Then, suddenly, he stepped up to it and bent over it.

"Don't touch that box!" she cried out.

But it was too late. His restless, trigger finger had already tapped on its side and sent the needle oscillating frantically.

They heard a low rumbling and, at first, the earth only grumbled. Yet even that was enough to loosen rocks and shake them off the awakened surface. But then the ground started to tremble, boulders came bounding down the canyon, whitish-yellow outcroppings smelling of sulfur. Maintaining his foothold on the ground as best he could, he gasped:

"You knew this would happen?!" he yelled through the

mounting rumble, dodging rocks and stones as best he could, "how did you know?!"

She took her time to answer.

"How did you know?!" He yelled again, more curious how she knew, than why the earth was quaking while rocks, barely missing their feet, tumbled down the mountainside.

"You saw the angels in the sky, didn't you?" she said at last.

"Fine, but how did you know this damn needle would set the ground in motion?"

"I heard the desert humming."

Slowly, the ground began to calm down, and the stones and rocks gradually rolled to a stop.

"What?!"

"I heard the desert humming."

"That's not it," he snapped brusquely, "that's just a sound in your ears, blood circulating. There must have been something else, something more."

He felt irritated. 'I've picked up some kind of a psychic weirdo along the way,' he thought, 'it was supposed to have been a simple trip to the desert.'

"There are no simple trips to the desert," she said.

"Hey, who are you anyway?!" he exclaimed. He grabbed her by the shoulders and lifted her. Only then did he realize how light she was. As he let go of her she fell slowly, like a petal, to the ground. And with that the earth finally calmed, one last rock rolled to a stop, one more piece of rubble for the alluvial fan.

Is it today or yesterday that this happened?' he wondered, 'a mirage of time, when a distant moment appears to be nearby.' He had no doubt about the place: close to the mouth of a dry canyon, where it begins to fan out into the valley. 'Thank god for that. Had it happened deep inside the canyon, we would have been pulverized.'

He suddenly felt tired and did not want to travel with her anymore. Until he met her, his ideas of how things were had been good companions and had left him at ease. But here was this new companion in the middle of the desert intruding into his psyche whom even Georgia O'Keeffe would not have been able to paint out of the picture.

"OK, tell me about the humming," he finally said, resigned to hear her out, and hoping she would pass over his grabbing her by the shoulders, "we'll talk about touching the box later." After all, she did seem attracted to him as they had floated in the hot spring before they entered the desert. 'Wouldn't that make her overlook such a minor misdemeanor?' he wondered as he remembered how her body glistened in the metallic sheen of the slippery, mineral-laden water.

But she would not be easily mollified.

"You want to slip and slide through my fingers—you're trying to make up, aren't you?" she said, "but the fact is, I have welts on my shoulders."

This was indeed a fact.

'Since we had arrived in this deadly place, it was another factual statement, besides the one on the semi-desert that she has made. I better hang on to this', Walter thought, 'or lose my sanity here, where donkeys knew no better than to wheel borax out of the valley below.'

"That was a long time ago," she said, "and they had no control over their fate."

"I don't seem to either," he said.

"Not if you cling to your ideas of how things are," she said

This sounded familiar, the old, family struggle—Annie striving for change and new ideas, while he and his son wanting things to stay as they were.

"I am trying not to cling," he finally said, "I did ask you about the humming, didn't I?"

She looked him in the eye.

"My shoulders still hurt," she said, then she sat on the ground and he did beside her.

He remembered the hot spring again. Her shoulders had been silky and pink, not a blemish on her whole body. Now she had two painful welts, one on each shoulder. They were beginning to hurt him too, branding his conscience. He knew she was waiting for an apology, but that would be too simple. He felt the need to explain so he decided to call upon the donkeys.

"What do you think would happen if the donkeys," he said, "as they pulled wagons full of borax, trekking along the valley, dragging their white dusty load, were suddenly startled by a humongous sneeze from one of the donkey-drivers?"

"They'd panic."

"And—perhaps kick the driver and give him welts?"

"Yes."

"Sorry I hurt you, but I panicked."

Having said this, he felt more in control, at last.

"Well, let's go." She was ready to get up and move on.

"Let's wait a bit," he suggested, "till you stop hurting." As he sat next to her, he longed to see her pink shoulders again and wish the welts away. Or, better still, to blow them gently away with the most ethereal of whispers. The gauze shawl hung over her shoulders, its brownish-gray blended with the color of the desert around them. He wished he could pull it aside and look.

"All right. I'd like to explain how I knew about the box, it was not the humming," she finally broke the silence, following her own trend of thought and ignoring his, "you said you wanted to hear about the box."

It was past high noon but the sun was still warming them, while over the desert below a mirage of air oscillated in waves of light and shadow.

"I was far away, in Guatemala," she began, "where Indian tribes still carry on their rites. There, roots of trees spread above ground and look like snakes in convolutions of love.

"One day I was walking around with a group of Indians. 'This is paradise' one of them said. 'But let's go further up, into the highlands,' he suggested. So we did."

She paused and hummed a tune from Atitlan. He felt a twinge of jealousy. 'Were there others before me wanting to take the shawl off her shoulders?' he wondered.

"Listen," she said, "I want to tell you how I knew about the box, but you must listen," she brought him up short.

"I don't remember whether it was morning or night," she went on, "probably morning or I would have seen the flickering of fires. The Indian led me by the hand. We walked between rocks and boulders, just like those here in this canyon, until high up in the hills we came upon an open space that had been cleared of rocks. There was no one around. In the center of the clearing and within a circle of stones a fire had been burning earlier, but now only hot charcoals were left. I was surprised to see the stones sparkle. I licked my finger, touched a stone and licked my finger again. It was sweet."

"What was it?" Walter asked. He could almost taste the sweetness of her fingers resting on the desert soil.

"Sugar," she said, "from sugar cane that they had grown themselves. Slash and burn, slash and burn, the sweet-smelling smoke drifting over the lowlands."

The tune from Atitlan hung over them in the air, and below them the fine dust of the Mojave.

"The Indians had sprinkled the sugar on the still burning embers," she continued, "on the ground, on the stones. 'To sweeten the gods,' the Indian said.

"I picked up a stick—quite casually, I don't know why. I felt the Indian tense up…"

She stopped for a moment and looked at the box. It lay quietly on the slope of an outcropping of limestone and sulfur, calmly asleep like a child after earth-rending cries and sobs.

"There was another scent mixing with that of burnt sugar," she went on.

"What was it?"

"Copal, it was copal, resin of the copal tree, burning like incense; it made everything more holy.

"Suddenly, I reached out and with my stick I touched the smoldering embers. The Indian grabbed my arm, pulled me to him and held me tight.

"'You shouldn't have done that!' he boomed over my head.

"But it was too late. There was a thundering blast right next to us, and another, and more in the distance. And with the thunder came rain, lashing down our bodies, gluing us together. This lasted only a minute or two but when it was over, the embers were just a gray puddle and the scent of incense was gone. And gone were all the other fires lit by the Indians this day and the night before.

"'Don't touch embers, not ever again, don't poke things you don't understand!' repeated the Indian, furious at me and at himself for not having been more watchful. He then waved me on and let me wander, all alone among the deadened ashes."

She fell silent and they watched the glow of the afternoon slowly change into a chilly dusk.

"And this is how I knew you shouldn't have touched the box," she said at last, "but I wasn't quick enough to stop you."

They sat quietly for a while, cushioned by silence. Suddenly a military plane flew by. Like a khaki shark, windowless, passing through the deep blue sky—the thought of his son Mark maybe up there—slowing down his thoughts.

He rose and extended his hand to help her up. They went slowly down the valley until they reached the middle of the Badlands.

"I'm thirsty," she said. There were a few drops of water left in the flask. He handed it to her.

"I had read that a man died of dehydration here last July," he said, "and they didn't find his body till December."

They stopped for a moment. He felt a gentle but constant blowing of air, drying the land of all vestiges of moisture. And silence, but for the sound of spiky brush and dark yellow grasses moving in unison in the currents of air, but for the echo of pebbles, still rattling in the distance. They listened.

"I hear the desert humming," he finally said.

She took his hand, they rose and moved on toward the black asphalt road that cut through the center of the valley.

Fear of Heights

She's waiting. She stops waiting, she will no longer wait, she's at the edge of a precipice, at the edge of the Grand Canyon.

She never had any fear of heights. As a teenager, visiting York Minster in York, England, she climbed the Central tower. Sneaking a look from the balustrade in between the balusters 235 feet down to the street below, caused her no fear or trepidation, only awe and excitement.

The push and pull of taking a jump from a height, at the edge of an edifice, of a precipice. How long would it take, she wonders, to jump from the edge of the Grand Canyon, about 6000 feet deep, to reach the ground below? About thirty seconds. How about a feather? If you drop a book and a pen from a tabletop at the same time, they reach the floor at the same time. This is not so in all circumstance and is governed by laws of physics. In order for them to hit the ground at the same time, she'd have to go into the rabbit hole of a vacuum. It would only then, during her fall, that she'd have the comforting sense of a kind of tapestry to catch her down below.

In reality, while dropping off the edge of the Canyon, she'd time to watch the layers that have formed the canyon wall over millennia from their beginning. A nanosecond flashback to a canapé she was once served in Paris—a layer of cream cheese, salmon and slice of cucumber on top not like any American sandwich that you gobble up between two slices of bread. No time for commas, the feather would still be floating by her side. On her way down she would notice a layer of seashells. Now she won't try to catch a twig because she knows her husband will have a canopy stretched below to catch her.

He's good at words so the canopy will be a tapestry of words. She's curious about the tapestry that she thought of in the rabbit hole. The English vocabulary has just over 170,000 words. Enough for a tapestry to serve as a safety net of 538 sq. feet. Depending of course on the style and the size of the font of the letters, the space separation between the lines must be minimal to make the net sturdy. Add colors—and her husband will have quite an attractive tapestry. Like a green canopy of trees, why not a canopy of words?

But why jump? Out of sheer curiosity, to test if she and a feather would drop simultaneously from a cliff and reach the bottom of the Canyon at the same time. But the Canyon is no vacuum and the test might fail.

Still, why jump at all? To counter and forever banish her fear of heights? The solution, if for some reason she misses the safety net, or her husband often prone to be late, is late setting it up.

Yet isn't there a pull, as much as a dread, to jump from a height? Something words can't convey?

She's at the edge.

She jumps.

She reaches the safety net—a trampoline—and bounces.

Her body keeps bouncing, bouncing, and bouncing.

He stands there, crying.

Drums

First day—nothing.

Second day—nothing.

Third day—something happened. The search in the jungle had been on all day but nothing was found until the hot mist lifted and finally many of the clues they were looking for appeared blatantly before their eyes. It made them wonder how earnestly they had looked, perhaps wary of finding those clues: branches of trees that had been bent by prevailing winds, now grotesquely woven together, saplings of trees intertwined and matted in their upward growth, tree trunks twisted in corkscrew fashion as if a giant and persistent tornado had exerted its omnipotent will.

Slowly and grimly the members of the investigation team arrived at the truth: a presence stronger than theirs had been at work here—except for a bumble bee that flew in once in a while, and they swatted it away.

A woman who had come with a research team a few months earlier was abducted from her bed, wrung out like a wet dish rag by a twisting force, tossed and deposited on the outskirts of the village. It was the current investigators' task to find out what had happened. They set up camp in a village where natives had lived in seemingly total ignorance of what went on in their vicinity.

Fourth day—nothing.

Fifth day. The members of the team tried to talk to the villagers. But the villagers did not want to talk to them. They were busy playing their drums. The few who agreed to talk had no useful information.

Sixth day—nothing.

Seventh day. The villagers were busy drumming their talking drums. Boomba, toomba, oom-ta-ta. The sound boomed, and swelled and reverberated. It set in motion air waves that oscillated higher and higher, stronger and stronger. The louder they drummed the higher the waves oscillated. All the villagers, from the oldest to the youngest held on to their talking drums and drummed.

Eighth day. Strange sensations went through the members of the team. First—a twitching of one finger, then another. A strand of hair lifting, then falling. First one of the team, then another seemed to lift off the ground, then was set down. The wind currents generated by the drumming grew stronger, then began to twist and pull three men and two women to the outskirts of the village. Suddenly there was a hissing sound and all five were sucked out of the village, wrung out like so many wet dish rags, then spewed out and deposited in the jungle in between the twisted saplings, contorted trees and branches, while the villagers held on to their drums, and drummed and drummed.

Nothing until the fourteenth day. One villager, dazed and confused by so many strangers walking about, stepped on a snake and drooped to the ground. A woman from the team leaned over him and tried to revive him with mouth to mouth resuscitation.

The other villagers approached the two aghast, then, with disgusted expressions on their faces they left. One of them ran to his hut and fetched a drum. Others followed suit and began to drum. *Boomba, toomba, oom-ta-ta.* The woman rose from the man she had been resuscitating, then seemed to be lifted off the ground against her own volition. The drumming became louder, there was a swishing sound. She was suddenly and rapidly spun on her axis, her face contorted—aaa! and she was gone.

The investigation team hurriedly left to file its report, but regardless of its findings, another team followed the following year.

The village could be reached through the jungle by a rutted path, in a rugged all-terrain vehicle, but preferably on a horse or a mule. Luke went as the leader of a research team to find out what had previously happened there. His interest was also to study drumming as it occurs in dance rhythm of the natives, in their processionals, and in their ritual funeral beats.

Against his recommendation for the research protocol, the villagers had to be subjected to a multiple question procedure, not in writing because they were illiterate but verbally. They became angry, then confused. They walked in circles, semi-stuporous, stepped on snakes and dropped dead, poisoned. The lianas that had earlier drooped airily, the gracefully shaped orchids, the vividly red, blue, and yellow birds that had flitted through the branches when his team arrived, gradually disappeared. Everything became dark, twisted and contorted, smelling of putrefaction and discontent.

The research was proceeding nevertheless. Luke tried to learn to play talking drums as the natives played them at their funerals. Friendly at first and teaching him the beat, the natives did not take kindly to all the concurrent questioning and enquiry. Then the situation turned grim. The villagers became restless while still oombing and boombing italicize these? on their drums. Toward the end of the project, three of Luke's men died of a mysterious food poisoning.

Luke should have cut the research short and returned home. And most certainly he should not have let his sweetheart, a woman from Oshkosh who came with him, to administer the multiple-choice exams. But this was the only thing she knew how to do. She was a student, inexperienced in other types of inquiry. Fascinated by drumming, she had often heard it as a dance rhythm, and here was her chance to research it in its various forms: as part of weddings, initiation ceremonials, and funeral rituals.

The multiple-choice questions went like this:
You play drums: yes, no?
Drumming is: good, bad, not good or bad?
Who drummed in your family: father, grandfather, great grandfather, none of them, all of them?
When you are drumming you feel: sad, happy, neither?
Drumming makes you: cry, smile, neither?

All respondents said they played drums, 'yes', drumming was 'not good or bad', their fathers, grandfathers, great grandfathers, 'all of them' had drummed, it made them feel 'neither', most not knowing what 'neither' meant, but said it just to get the woman off their backs. After the exam they seemed dazed, they stepped on snakes as they had never done before.

Was this kind of inquiry worth the aggravation it had cause? Luke wondered. Yet it had to be done, it was part of the research protocol. Protocol! It made him mad that he was not allowed to drop the procedure, which he had to follow it.

The nights seemed never to end. Usually Luke did not sleep well; he felt that the darkness played into the hands of something evil, unfamiliar to him. But then the dawn would come, and all concerns would be pushed aside. Until the day of the bumble bee. It had arrived from God knows where. It buzzed and buzzed around everyone's ears, the researchers', as well as the natives'. It was bad luck to kill a bumble bee, everyone put up with it, yet everyone had become increasingly tired and irritated, including the natives. When night came everyone fell into bed, exhausted. That is, almost everyone. Luke stayed half-awake, and he thought he heard sounds and whispers around his hut, but then a high wind rose, he thought no more about it and fell asleep. When he awoke in the morning his sweetheart was gone. She was later found dead on the outskirts of the village. The natives took up their drums, and drummed, and drummed *oomba-toomba, oom-ta-ta*, the funeral beat all day.

Every time a funeral caravan files now through the streets of Oshkosh it does so at a markedly reduced speed because, at the end of it there is a man following it slowly, with a stoop, his long, bedraggled hair drooping round his face. He walks with a sluggish, halting gait. His left arm encircles a talking drum, and with his right hand he beats the funeral rhythm *oomba-toomba, oom-ta-ta*.

Noises were Coming

Ahmed was his name.

*   *   *

It had been an intense time out in the Orient, mosquitos everywhere, and Christa had contracted malaria. Now back home and recovered, she was besieged by noises coming from everywhere, from trees, electric lines overhead, from an underground broken water pipe that had caused a sinkhole. They were not what you might call ubiquitous noises, she tried to but was unable to localize them and became exhausted. She finally realized that they were coming from her anguished psyche.

They were not what she wanted to hear, a phone call from Kurt would be a welcome relief, but she hadn't heard from him for three days. Their relationship not passionate, they mostly stayed at home, at his place or hers, and led a quiet life. Kurt didn't like to dance but they went anyway to those halls under glittering lights, the music swirling the dancers around. Christa was an excellent dancer, and she knew how to submit to any man taking a lead. She knew how to be pulled into a tight embrace that would meld their torsos and all the way down to their legs. But now her dancing shoes sat restlessly under her chair. So she watched other couples, their torsos tightly linked or, when more distant, their eyes saying more than anything words could convey.

Finally the phone call came:

"Hello, I have news for you!" Kurt said.

"What is it, you sound like you're out of breath."

"Yes, my wife finally had her baby!"

"So?"

"What do I do about it?"

"Love it, of course."

"But, but it's not mine!"

"What do you mean?"

"I haven't had sex with Becky for over a year."

"So whose is it?"

"I don't know. But there is more, I hate to tell you."

"Just go ahead."

"It's deformed."

"How?"

"It has hands only as far as the elbows. A lot of screaming here, sounds of despair everywhere!"

"Oh, m'god! Wait. I'll come over and you'll tell me all about it."

On her way, there were no noises, except now in her head 'hands at its elbows, hands at the elbows.' It was a wintery afternoon, the black ice not yet cleared from the roads, the wheels of her Chevy skidding once or twice. She had to slow down.

"So what happened?" On her arrival it was Christa the one out of breath.

"I never told you, but there was some abnormality showing on radiographic imaging one third into her pregnancy."

"How about abortion?"

"Becky wouldn't have it."

"Sanctity of life… but we kill mosquitoes when they try to bite us."

"Don't be ridiculous."

"A mosquito bite is certainly less trouble—or is it, considering some disease it might convey—than an unwanted or deformed child. And what does the father say?"

"He's nowhere to be found. A prince from Mesopotamia or something."

"Where is Mesopotamia?"

"Somewhere in the Orient, between the rivers Tigris and Euphrates."

'Yes… Ahmed was his name…, somewhere on the banks of the Euphrates…'

"That's a great help. But… but how did this happen?"

"Something I never told you. Becky had been taking thalidomide during her pregnancy for morning sickness… from Brazil… what a tragedy. You're right—she's one of those who believe in the sanctity of life, and she refused abortion."

"So what will you do now?"

"I'll stay with the kid."

"And with his mother?"

"Yea… sure…"

Noble and righteous as it was obvious to Christa, she suddenly felt pangs of pain and jealousy, from her unconsciousness and bloom like forgotten weeds. Her ears clamped down at the dance hall next time they went there, she no longer wanted to hear the music or any other noises. Kurt had compassion for the child to quell his angst, while she wanted none of hers. She picked up her pocketbook and left.

Left for what? For the barren walls of her room, which would bounce an echo of Kurt's phone calls, should they ever come. Or, perhaps, of the benevolent sounds and noises of train rides with mommy, *troo-boo-boo-boom*, which had been calming her childhood wails.

It now occurred to her that rides on the insides and undersides of freight train carriage might do the same. Not being a mosquito to be slapped away by Kurt, she decided to became a hobo, like the little-known Mrs. Soper over a century ago, and may women since that time.

She found the right garb in a dumpster discarded on one of the streets downtown, also dirty worn out, baggy pants, a ripped shirt smelling of sweat. She fumigated and laundered them, left the rips intact. She cut her hair short and put on a hat with a visor also from a dumpster, which she had also washed, and set it at a perky angle on her head to counter the misery still gnawing her. Perhaps she'd smudge her face with dirt so you wouldn't know from her expression that some unremitting tissue was constricting her heart from exploding.

In case she might also need something more appropriate as normal street wear, she packed a tunic-like shirt, colorful but simple, of light cotton, picked up some time ago at a market on her way home through Bagdad, all easily packed into a small, compressible backpack. No need to cut her hair to very short to hide her female gender.

Time passed from that slippery day on her way to Kurt. By next fall she was on a country road lined by trees whose leaves have not yet but soon would turn orange and red, also between fields of rolled hay stacks that gave her some solace. Finally she reached a freight trains depot. One of the train doors were open and, making sure no one was watching, she hopped in. She was soon joined by one, then two male hobos.

"How are ya, miss?" one of them asked.

"Fine."

"Are ya familiar or new at this?" another asked.

"New."

"Aaa!"

The train started moving slowly, with a low and heaving sound.

"We know the place where it will stop and they open the doors to unload somethin', pr'aps boxes of dry goods. We hide in a corner here, then come out when the doors close. Are ya with us?"

"Yup."

"Not dun riding yet under train carriages?"

"Of course not."

"Ya'll learn. But don't try the undercarriage routine too soon. Practice at a depot."

Christa pulled out a bag of trailmix out of her tiny backpack and shared it with them.

"Thanks, that's nice. Too bad we can't go on with ya as we have to hop out at the next stop."

For some time they chugged on in silence, the train doing its sounds and noises.

And so she went, at first alone, then with other hobos, hopping in and out of trains, but mostly those that were just beginning to move.

"Next place is a small town and we have to skip it. Too many 'knows-it-alls' and they might recognize us hobos," one of the hobos remarked.

When the train stopped near that town Christa jumped out. She hid down a levy, and changed into her shirt.

Walking along the main street, she stopped by a store that sold sneakers. Inside, they gave her water, a milkshake, something more substantial and coffee if she cleaned their counters.

Then back on another train.

After a few miles she sensed the train slowing down with a low, rumbling sound, stopping, doors opening to a view of a bigger town. She left this train and waited for the next one, or one after that, and then went on to other small towns, some with one-room schoolhouses, others with none where inhabitants taught their kids in one half of their church basements or carter them to neighboring towns.

A woman clerk at one of the drugstores was curious about Christa and her travels.

"Where are ya' from?" she asked.

"Oh, all over the place."

"Ya' must know a lot about the wide world. That funny shirt you're wearing…"

"Not really."

She later changed again into her bobo outfit and went, alone or with other hobos, hopping in and out of trains. Most of the hobos were not in the least surprised when they saw a woman among them.

Any time the train stopped she would jump out and explore the adjacent town.

Walking along one of the main streets, she remembered the kind of small towns she'd seen on her trips with Kurt. This memory, she now realized, was fading and no longer irked her.

Looking through the glass door of a drugstore she saw a soda counter. She went in asked for a glass of water. It sold everything from shoelaces to napkins to cheap kitchen utensils. Its pharmacy section would carry only the most commonly used drugs such as those for high cholesterol and high blood pressure. Their supply would last for a week, she was told, until their itinerant doctor re-ordered the supply. Farther down the street there was a convenience store with something more substantial to eat than what remained out her trailmix, but she was afraid to miss the departure of her train, so she hopped back in.

After a few miles she sensed the train slowing down, stopping, doors opening to a view of a bigger town. She decided to leave this train and wait for the next one.

She managed to get cheap lodging right downtown. This time she did find a convenience store that served fresh subs on demand, and also coffee from a machine. Luckily there was an ATM for cash she got with her credit card. She ordered a big sub with beef, cheese, tomato and lettuce. It replenished her for the moment and for next couple of days.

Chitchatting with the owner she found out that he was no stranger to visitors and even hobos.

"Yes, these come in ones or twos and sit outside on my doorsteps."

"Are there many still around?" She asked.

"Not here, but if you go north to Canada there is even a chap there, St. Pierre that's made a study of them."

"Yes, I've heard of him."

"But would you believe it, those here in the States have a convention in Bitt, Iowa, every year in August."

"Really?"

"Thank god we have no Gypsies here."

"Oh, are there any in the US?"

"Yes, in southern states like Louisiana, southern California, Texas."

Going up to the cold north in Canada was not to her liking,

so she spent more time hopping on trains through the Midwest, North and South Dakotas. This being already September she missed the convention in Bitt. 'Some other time perhaps,' she thought.

*   *   *

As the earth turned from fall to winter, then to spring and summer, and rotated round the sun a few times, years passed. By now Christa was almost forty and no longer nimble about hopping onto freight trains. Her days of bumping and jerking and lonely nights under skies, gray from billions of stars, constellations, the Milky Way and other galaxies became now like the smudge she had declined to smear on her face. Missing skips onto trains, and having her scratches that got infected to be treated at some outlying ER lost its exotic charm. But she didn't feel like returning home just yet.

'How about a change in direction?' she pondered, 'instead of east to west and back again as freight trains seem to run, how about north to south and back up again? Buses ran that way.' During her stays in motels, by now most of them had a TV, Christa busied herself by touring the internet. She checked information about Gypsies down south and found out that they may have originated in India, then migrated to Europe, mainly to Romania, hence their other name Roma. They arrived in the US, some as slaves, in the 1800s or even earlier, and perhaps because of the warm climate settled mostly in the southern states. Otherwise they too would have been crisscrossing America's vastness, like Christa had done.

'Thank god we have no Gypsies here,' she remembered the store owner saying. She would now become a nomad, not like the actress horsewoman Julia Roberts, who rode wild horses with the nomads in Mongolia, but on foot with the Gypsies, if they were moving.

Still with access to some cash Christa clicked on an ATM and bought another shirt, she was now ready to take buses south.

After many changes and sleeping in motels she arrived in Memphis. For some people, this city had an uncomfortable association because, if they happened to know, it and its Mississippi to Arkansas bridges in particular, had been the sites of many unsolved deaths.

Tragic as the deaths had been, some of their causes were solved, others were not. Exploring this, as well as towns big and small while still a hobo, could have been great material for a writer's pen. But a writer she was not, and she had to move on.

On her way south Christa had to cross one of these long bridges, stomping the deaths underfoot. But she couldn't 'stomp' so to speak, so she got a ride by a kindly driver over of one of the bridges; he didn't ask her any questions and she would not be interested in his answers.

After a few more rides, she reached the border to Louisiana and crossed it. Here, by word of mouth, she received directions to the most likely locations where she might find Gypsies.

However, what interested Christa the most was their music. She had known it and loved it for many years and had been an admirer of Django Reinhardt. He was born to a Romani family in Belgium and had become world famous for his Gypsy-inspired guitar music.

Christa found a Gypsy encampment not far from the border. She approached it gingerly, not knowing what kind of reception she would get, especially not familiar with their language. However, she thought that two words would give her an entry. She waited in the vicinity, and when she saw a few people wandering about, she timidly said to one of the men:

"Django Reinhardt…?"

It worked. She was invited to join them for their midday meal and, since some of them had already been familiar with English, they expressed pleasure and surprise that a white woman had an interest in visiting them. However, she was disappointed that most of them had become "Americanized." They had been settled in an encampment of cabins and cabin cruisers, wearing tee-shirts, some even suits, hardly leading a nomadic life, sometimes only driving around in their cruisers for a change of scenery. She would now be alone, carrying the weight of her filmy shirt inside her bra and her disappointment on the back of her shoulders.

After a few days of mingling the Gypsies invited her to one of their musical events of guitar playing, dancing, then to a few more. As an excellent dancer, she used her way of becoming soft and submissive while following any man's lead and, as she'd be wont to do, letting him pull her into a tight embrace.

But in her lonely cabin where were her loves of yesteryear? Then slowly, passions aroused again, Christa fell in love with one of the men. Was it their darkish olive skin all the way from India… or *from the Tiger and Euphrates…* then to Europe and to the States? She began to dream about the Gypsy man nights, and spent most of her days following him with her eyes wherever he went. At first, no one paid much attention, it was just her white woman's way, they thought, though they noticed her passionate style of dancing, especially with this man. His name was Vano.

As weeks dragged on Christa noticed that something began to happen: women took to whispering among themselves, then they shunned her and eyed her with hostile looks.

One morning, waking from a deep sleep and stepping outside her cabin, Christa found her meager possessions bundled on her doorstep, with a note attached:

PLEASE LEAVE.

She left, but not before something pressing must have, had to be done. Later at night she heard Vano's snoring in a neighboring cabin, she quietly snuck inside it, softly kissed his hand and did something which would embroil her in horror but also achieve redress until the end of her days.

Back in her cabin she changed her clothes into her hobo garb and left into the darkness of the night.

Next morning, when Vano was late for the communal breakfast one of the men went to awaken him. There was a howl that no one had ever heard before. Everybody rushed to Vano's place, saw him covered in blood and no longer breathing. The first suspicion fell on one of the vagabonds always wandering near their site. There was yelling and searching, yet they were reluctant to call the police for fear that the law would fault one of their own.

A long time elapsed before someone realized that Christa was missing, they called the police, but time enough for Christa to have crossed the border and beyond their jurisdiction.

No further action was taken.

Why?

Because Vano was 'only' a Gypsy.

The upper echelons lost interest in a crime of passion, which they still had in France. But the edict read: *We do not advocate murdering children (as we know from our history of antecedents Medea had done to avenge her beloved Jason's desertion), but in this case we do accord leniency a place for a crime of passion.*

*   *   *

On her return home a year or so later, and after her first breakfast at a counter, Christa walked downtown. Not much had changed. Stopping at her usual convenience store to buy bread, she noticed on a board of announcements that there was going to be a concert that night, of classical music at the church she had occasionally visited in her earlier days. 'Strange, classical music in that church,' she thought, but, having nothing to do on her first night home, she decided to attend it.

After buying a somewhat formal blouse and skirt and after a leisurely day of settling in a temporarily rented room, she headed for the church. She sat in one of the back pews, looked around but did not see any familiar faces. The orchestra was already seated at the altar end of the church and the audience in a deep hush.

A teenager, maybe sixteen years old, came out of the vestry. There was something odd about him, she couldn't quite see from the distance, but was surprised that he wore a short-sleeve shirt—this she could see—for an evening performance. When he stepped up to the podium, turned around to greet the audience and to receive its enthusiastic clapping, she saw his arms: they were only elbow-long. The boy then turned to the orchestra and they began playing their first piece, slow but engaging, slow and sweetly sounding, conducted by a teenager with hands at his elbows.

Christa listened for a while, but couldn't concentrate and again looked around. Someone was looking at her... Kurt in one of the front pews, smiling, then a man next to him, turning to her with a smile of surprise and recognition... his face, presumably the father of the boy.

She first met him on the banks of the Tigris or was it Euphrates? Standing erect, his face into the wind and sand, her skirt billowing in the wind, in the distance tops of palm trees swayed by the same wind. Then nights on the sand, no mosquito netting, mosquitoes let flying (thank god no tsetse fly bites or she would have slept through it all), malaria fevers coming and going, coming and going, the sound of his voice always there. Then silence.

Christa did not stay to the end of the performance. The noises, wails and cries over stilted arms returned. A week later, in another town, a neighboring town, she got a job of a clerk in a bank. On her way to work she would remove the bangles from her wrists from that other time, or they'd be in the way on her cashier's counter. She stayed at home, listening to noises, noises of silence of her solitude.

There was a knock on the door, she opened it, and there he stood. Ahmed was his name.

The Zebra

With one foot in the grove and the other in the abbey Daniel hoped that his prayer would be heard. He placed a piece of chalk under a beech tree and waited for the zebra to come by. The entire evolution passed before his right eye as it remained fixed on a point in the distance. He had lost the left eye in the Agrarian Conflict and it had been replaced with a glass marble. So poised, he waited for the arrival of the zebra.

Daniel had seen many zebras in the past, so many that he had lost count of their stripes. But there was one that reappeared in his dreams. She was wrapped like a swaddling in layers of string and ribbon. It would take an eternity to unravel the wrapping and reveal the circular and parallel stripes on her rotund body and sinewy legs. On awakening he hoped and prayed that someday she would appear to him in her nascent state, like a babe out of swaddling cloth, totally unwrapped.

Daniel conceived his wish long before the Agrarian Conflict, while he was still a child and had two eyes with which to count stripes. His mother was alive then. For her, life was a design. She walked in circles, she talked in circles. She wore dresses that were striped, she wore her hair in stripe-like tresses. Comma splices in these last two sentences?

"Most of life is in stripes—yes circular and parallel," she used to say.

One day she promised her seven-year-old son something for Christmas that would show him what she meant. But long before Christmas the child wanted to know.

"What is circular, mommy, what is parallel?"

"Some people, for example, walk in circles, or way off in parallels that never meet," she did her best to explain.

"Circular ways are fine, my boy, but I think that parallel ones are better."

"And what does daddy think?" asked the child, still befuddled.

"I don't know. Ask him."

But he never did. And when Christmas came, there was a toy zebra under the tree.

"Isn't she beautiful—striped in circles and in parallels?" mommy ooed and cooed italics over the zebra, hoping the child would be equally happy. She was crazy of course and lived in the isolation of her thinking.

The following winter, just before Christmas, weakened by severe weather and debilitated by her craziness she caught flu that turned her cheeks the color of heliotrope. After that Daniel never saw her again, and whenever he wondered where his mommy was, he was shown an oblong mound of dirt which, to his little boy's eyes, seemed enormous and a strange place to be under.

'When I grow up,' he thought, 'I'll be big and strong and dig mommy out.'

In her short span of life she managed to leave an indelible imprint on her child: a fancy for zebras and for stripes. Circular ones that would go round and round, parallel ones that would never meet. 'Was this what she had in mind'—the 'never meet' of eternal solitude?' Daniel wondered as he grew into manhood.

At the eruption of the Agrarian Conflict all stripes of imagination had to be set aside, because the Conflict surpassed all imagination. Daniel's left eye was avulsed. He was about to be deprived of his sight entirely so he would not bear witness to all that was happening but, just as his captors were reaching for his right eye, there was banging and yelling and shooting. The captors panicked and took off, and Daniel was rescued. Eventually the cavity of his left eye healed.

When the Conflict was over nothing was left but ruins and mounds of rubble. What had been agricultural land was now wasteland. A few groves of beech and prune trees survived and these, in Daniel's one-eyed vision, were now romping grounds for zebras.

Daniel wandered about like a shadow of his former self, a bony figure dressed in rags and paper bags. 'The Agrarian Conflict had come to an end with a resolution that left no one out, and satisfied no one,' he thought. His left eye had been replaced with a glass marble, and he could still see, with his other eye, zebras romping in the groves.

His reports of this phenomenon did not disturb anyone because it was not of their doing, and what was not of their doing required no explanation. He wandered about fields counting stripes that farmers were making with tractors while plowing their fields. The mound of dirt under he which his mommy was put to rest years ago was ever on his mind. But he felt that he first needed to re-enter the mainstream of life. As far as he could see, there were mounds everywhere that had been covered with turf and resembled ordinary hillocks. Most of them were now topped with buildings, two or three, sometimes even more. And for now, it was these mounds that evoked his curiosity and called for his attention. So he bought himself a trowel.

The day was green, green with grass, green with foliage, green with light reflecting from the grass and seeping through the leaves. Daniel sat on the slope of one such mound, took out his trowel and pushed it into the ground. At first the turf gave way easily. He scraped it away. He then tried to push deeper, but to no avail. The tip of his trowel was hitting something that felt and sounded like cement. 'Cement? If only I could dig deeper with a bigger tool!' Daniel sighed. He bought himself a spade.

"What are you doing with that spade, man?" people asked, "you can't just walk about and dig without permission. You want the 'mainstream of life,' you say, well here it is: permits, people's rights, privacy, rights to eminent domain. You're walking the landscape in your dirt-gray, baggy clothes, and scaring everyone with your spade!"

"Alright, alright," Daniel replied, "I'll knock on people's doors and ask permission."

The next several days Daniel spent knocking on doors. "No, you can't dig here, I've just planted my garden," one woman said. "Wash up, get new clothes, something spiffier, you know, and look for a regular job," another told him. One man, afraid of government intrusion made him read part of a chapter of the law, #6658:

> Any person or persons claiming that an estate
> freehold in wild lands or in an interest in common
> and undivided therein ... may maintain an action
> to quiet or establish the title thereto or to remove
> a cloud from the title thereto.

"See," the man said, "I may maintain an action to quiet or to remove a cloud, if you plan to tinker or tamper with this piece of my estate."

But eventually a few people gave him permission to dig. At first all he found was soil and pieces of cement, but, as he began to dig deeper, he extracted plastic cups, bits of charred steak. Other items had to be eased out and pulled out slowly: a baby's diaper, scraps of clothing.

Daniel found variations in the garbage depending on local preferences—there were no babies' diapers where discarded condoms predominated, there was no meat offal where the bulk of garbage consisted of vegetable off-cuts. 'But... is all this stuff non-degradable?' Daniel wondered in amazement and asked the question of a passer-by.

"Yea, man, all those condoms," the man said, misunderstanding the thrust of Daniel's question, "during the Conflict there must have been some huge explosion here in the middle of a big fuck." They both knew the heightened urge to copulate during times of war. "But there must also be bones somewhere," the fellow added as an afterthought.

"Yes… but what I mean is… my question is… how is it that the garbage has not disintegrated? How does it stand up to the weight of buildings, to children jumping up and down, to people thumping in beds, to housewives pounding dough for bread?"

"Well, they added steel and cement of course. Garbage mixed with soil, reinforced with steel and cement doesn't disintegrate—it just doesn't."

"And bones, you said, there must be bones…"

"Yea, lots of those somewhere, from the time of the Conflict."

"I haven't found any yet."

Daniel traveled on until one day he saw a hill rising out of a wide-sweeping plain. Coming up closer he saw a grove of prune and beech trees. Weary and lonely, he would have liked to walk among the trees and look for zebras. He would have liked to nuzzle against their glistening black and white exteriors, to be welcomed and caressed after his long journey.

He looked at the hill again. It was a mound. In its enormous size it was unlike any he had seen so far, on the arid landscape of his middle years. Like none, that with measured steps he had trod around and scraped and dug for those non-perishable goods and was left with more and more questions still unanswered. The mound was oblong and its slopes rose smoothly to a flattened surface at the top. And there stood, he could see from the distance, not just a few buildings, but a whole city, like a medieval fort. But there was no moat, no ancient wall to cross, no heavy iron gate to open. Beyond the mound, by the grove of beeches, he saw some jagged ruins of an abbey which had not been totally razed during the Conflict.

Daniel slowly climbed the mound, and when he reached the top he headed straight for the city square. No one was around at first but gradually, in ones and twos, a few people gathered. With glassy looks they eyed his one-eyed face and did not seem eager to welcome him. But Daniel had been curious for too long to be put off from asking them some questions.

"Is this city built on a mound?"

"Yes," they said.

"Did it exist before the Conflict?"

"No."

"And the mound?"

"No, not the mound either."

"May I dig on the side of the mound?"

"No."

And that was that, and no more was said. They walked away in silence.

One season passed, then another. First, yarrow lost its bloom, then queen Anne's lace lost its lace. The nights grew long, the sky was gray, and the moon had not been seen for over a month. Winter was coming and digging would be hard.

The day Daniel decided to leave, he sat in the city square with his few belongings tied to his back, counting cracks in the pavement that would lead him out of the city, when a group of people—looked like a delegation—came up to him. They settled around him on small, wooden-legged canvas folding stools that they had brought for the occasion. After much hesitation and prodding of one another—

"How did you lose your eye?" one of them asked.

'The devil curse their question,' Daniel thought, and he fell into a silence of his own... 'But perhaps they need to know?'

"It was during the Agrarian Conflict," he began, "they held me by my limbs and with a small, sharp scoop…"

"Yes, yes, that's all we need to know. You had obviously suffered like we all did…"

They huddled and whispered among themselves until two older men came forward, and brought out a spade and a pitchfork from behind their baggy, dark-brown trousers.

"Here," they said, "go, dig and look."

Early next morning, frost was still on the ground, Daniel went outside the city, and then to the side of the mound. A few men and women followed him in a small procession. Setting to work he dug into the soil. Quickly at first, but he soon slowed down—

and not because the ground was hard.

There was none of the usual fare of garbage previously known to him in mounds. There were no food scraps.

"There was nothing to eat," he was told, "toward the end of the conflict."

No yarn or fabric goods.

"We had hardly any clothes to wear, not even in winter." What he did find were bits of charred flesh, a mop of a child's hair, a woman's broken pelvis, a piece of chalk someone had nibbled on for calcium. This he carefully wrapped in tissue and placed in his pocket. Then, turning to the people he hesitatingly said:

"But you built your city on sacred ground… Why had you not cleared the ruins, why did you build on top of the bodies? This should have been a burial site."

"We knew we were building on sacred ground," they replied, "but there was too much to clear, too few of us left alive, all weak and tired."

"So what did you do?"

"…winter was coming, we needed shelter, so we built houses. The following spring we cleared the land below and around the mound, and planted trees."

"How did you manage to build on top of what was there?"
"You've dug and poked us enough!" one of them exclaimed, "do you want to know how much rubble we used per what area? how many steel girders to how many broken bones? how many bricks and how much cement to how many bodies, adult or children?!"

"Good God, no!'

"May God strike you dead if you ask much more," said a small gray woman in a wheelchair whose back had been broken and reset under force during the Conflict. Through zigzag thoughts and jagged memories Daniel visualized the parallels of mounds he had seen before. He decided to ask no more and went on digging

Word spread of Daniel's excavation, and reporters flocked to the scene.

"Do you use gloves, Mr., as you shovel the dirt and all the

items in it?" they asked.

"Yes, and forceps and tweezers too, sometimes a knife and a fork," Daniel's irritation grew at their probing, "rarely a dessert spoon!" he snapped at their intrusiveness.

The excavation was on everyone's lips, and Daniel himself became obsessed with it. He went on digging and grinding horror into his bones. But when he pulled out a piece of tram rail, a wheel, a coupling, buried memories came alive. He remembered traveling in a trolley through an area that had, under orders, been isolated from the rest of the city. All tram stops had been cancelled there. Through a window he saw frightened faces, he saw arms raised in parallel, pleading and stretching to the heavens in terror and in rage. And now, these memories, compressed by time into a dark space, passed through his mind, ready to explode.

Out of these images of the past, suddenly, parallel configurations (just as mommy had said, God rest her soul) crowded his sickened spirit, overwhelming him with an urge to search for zebras in the groves, to be comforted by mommy as she used to lean over him while he was in his bed and going to sleep, whispering to him in a soft voice, that circular stripes are beautiful, and parallel ones the most beautiful of all. He also remembered sitting at a big table, he was about seven, pouring over books with pictures of animals. It was just before Christmas, when suddenly he came upon a picture of a zebra. Her bulging rump was all in stripes, black and white. He showed it to his mother. 'Is this what you mean, mommy?' he asked.

When Christmas came there was a gift under the tree, wrapped in many layers of colorful strings and ribbons. He sat on the floor unraveling it all, and, by the time everyone had unwrapped all their gifts, he had unwrapped only part of his. It seemed like an eternity. But finally, out of reams and reams of ribbon emerged a toy zebra, real fur, soft, smooth and shiny, in stripes of the most beautiful black and white. He held it and cuddled it, and mommy was so happy that he liked the zebra. It did not matter anymore how long he spent unwrapping it, but just the same, he asked:

"Please, mommy, next Christmas, can my gift come already unwrapped?"

She seemed upset: "Oh, I put so much effort into this special Christmas wrapping, circular and parallel," she said, but she promised to fulfill his wish.

"Will it help to pray?"

"Perhaps."

The following December, it was an unusually cold one, she caught the flu, and she passed away just before Christmas. 'Is it my fault she ended up under a mound?' the child whimpered in tears and bewilderment.

It was all so hazy and long ago, that first Christmas of his memories. Another day, another Christmastime. He left the mound momentarily to visit the grove of prunes, and returned from there with a pair of tongs; he had used them to pick prunes which he would offer the zebras at their next encounter. He was now back at the mound and was digging where the surface seemed particularly hard. However, a few vigorous bangs with the handle of the tongs loosened the ground in one small area and made the soil crumble, opening up a small chamber. He pushed the tongs and his arm as far as his elbow. Feeling around with the tongs, he pulled out a tangled mass of cloth the size of an infant. 'Had it been a swaddling?' he wondered. Reams and reams of bands of cloth, now turned dirty-gray, may have been wrapped around a new-born babe; all that was left were strands of cloth and bones, incompletely filling what must have been a gaping space.

'If a gift ever came from hell, this would have been it,' Daniel thought.

He placed the bundle back in its cavern, pushed back the soil, and left.

The morning sun had long since dispelled the mysteries of the night. Daniel slowly approached the grove that bordered on the abbey. The zebra, which he now hoped and prayed to see with his one-eyed vision would not be like any one of those he had seen before, romping in the grove. She would be more beautiful, her rump more shiny and vividly striped, a flush of heliotrope at her nostrils.

He remembered the piece of chalk he had picked up from the mound. It was still in his pocket. He took it out of the tissue and placed it carefully under the wide-branching beech tree, hoping that if he laid it just at the right place the zebra would come.

Although still wrapped in strings and ribbons she would not wait for him but would shed them all by herself. He would then know that his prayer has been heard.

The Smog

The prevailing winds blow the smog from Greece in the north to the Dodecanese islands in the south. A brownish haze hangs over the Aegean Sea, even as far southeast as the mountains and the seemingly deserted Turkish coast. The shoreline of Rhodes in this archipelago is covered with flat-tumbled, oval beach stones. The sea close to the coast is cerulean blue.

Occasionally, between one wave and another, a trickle of blood appears then disappears.

She first saw the smog as she flew over the Greek island of Rhodes. To her surprise it was worse than anywhere else, billowing in brown clouds and spreading as far as the Turkish coast, a few miles across the Aegean Sea. After she stepped off the plane and reached her destination, it took her no time to unpack and settle in. She then went for a long walk along the shore, and in the ensuing days she walked the pavements of the town of Rhodes.

All her life she wanted to do good, to do the right thing. She didn't yet know how, so she let Puzzo, her first boyfriend, stick to her like a piece of chewing gum under a tabletop, where her fingertip would hit upon it.

Being with Puzzo was hard. His language was obscure, and the only time she understood him was when he pointed his finger to the bed. That was good but not good enough. When their date was over, she would give him his shoes and ask him to leave.

Deep down she hated those shoes. Although they were of supple Brazilian leather, crafted with skilled Brazilian workmanship, they came to a point that was now out of fashion; they also marked Puzzo as South American. She didn't mind that too much, but her preference had always been for the Greek

Adonis type of man. She had admired the Greek statues in the museums she visited. Looking at the fig leaf and thinking about what it was hiding was always the source of titillation.

Puzzo smoked a lot, and here at least she thought she could do some good. She began with small things: she gave him a disappointed look when he flipped cigarette ashes on the floor, a little cough when his smoke drifted in her direction. But he didn't understand her fussing. On their visit to Greece together, he would indicate with a wide sweep of his arm that everyone smoked here, so perhaps he did understand what she had been trying to convey to him.

Everyone! Here was something good to be done, if it wasn't too late. Brown clouds of smoke billowed into the sky, the air smelled acrid. No one else seemed to notice, not even that their skin was turning brown. They must have been suffering from color-blindness, she thought, and had lost their sense of smell. Or they didn't care. In an attempt to do good and save at least one human being, she turned her attention to Puzzo.

"Acrid, acrid," she said to him one evening, pointing to her nose and sniffing the bad-smelling air.

He didn't understand and picked up a dictionary to look up the word.

"Bitter… bitter?" he said in puzzlement and, attempting to turn matters in a more pleasant direction, he pointed his finger to the bed.

"Well, at least this isn't bitter," she said and surrendered.

The Greek statues that she had seen in museums had been returning to her mind. As in the museums, so in her dreams they were alabaster white. After some time she gave up on Puzzo, and decided to go alone to the land where the models for these statues came from.

She already saw smog, as her plane was on its approach to one of the Greek islands she had chosen to visit. To her surprise it was worse than what she had expected, billowing in brown clouds and spreading as far as the Turkish coast, a few miles across the Aegean Sea.

After she stepped off the plane and reached her destination, it took her no time to unpack and settle in. She then went for a long walk along the shore, and in the ensuing days she walked the pavements of the town of Rhodos. It took a light step and an easy mind to do that.

At first, the native people thought she had both, until she began to address their men sitting in the town's cafés, with uneasy gestures.

She noticed that their skin was hardly alabaster white. These men seemed to sit for hours, drinking coffee, smoking cigarettes, one after another, their hands busy moving komboloi, the worry beads. Thinking they might be worried about the smog, she pointed her finger to the sky and wondered if that was it. But communication was hard. As with Puzzo, their language was obscure. They shook their heads and, no, that's nothing, they seemed to say.

She then pointed to the mosaics on the pavements of the town. They were made of tumbled, flat beach stones. She indicated as best she could that they should have portrayed not just flowers and leaves but also birds in flight, people and animals on the run. That's what she thought.

No, tell this little stringla, Greek for vixen, there is no need to run, people seemed to say. There's nothing wrong, they seemed to repeat, and she heard annoyance in their voices. They made ready to take off their shoes and throw them at her.

One day she went to the beach. She watched a man as he spread his towel on the ground, he stretched it, pulled at it here and there, set a couple of stones on each corner. Why does the man fuss so much, she wondered? He must be worried about the afternoon wind due to rise any moment, it occurred to her. When it arrives, it will turn over chairs and tables, bend trees in one direction and, over time, the trees will stay that way.

The man finally stood up. He had the body of an Adonis—no mistaking him for Puzzo. But instead of alabaster-white like in the museums, his body was the color of soot. He went for a swim.

That's good, she thought, feeling a tingle in her toes. Someday I too will go into this water, she thought. She watched a brownish haze hanging low over the water. The sky was blue and clear high above, which is why the men had said there was nothing wrong here.

Later that day she went to a store to buy food. While laying out her goods at the cashier's, she was trying to tell the women about the soot she saw everywhere, even on the counters of the store. Why don't you just pay attention to your groceries, you little twit, their angry looks seem to say. Did they think I was after their men earlier that day, she wondered.

These women will not be sorry when they see a trickle of blood between the waves…

Next day they gathered outside her window. Their words were muddled phrases and she didn't understand their meaning. She felt her heart beat and thump as she pressed her body against the backrest of her armchair, listening. Should she come out and protest, try to say something? When they were finally gone, she left the house and walked out onto the street. Two dogs, set on her by the women, ran after her, barking. A shaggy mutt and a rottweiler. They snarled, bared their teeth and snapped at her legs. She tried to calm them, but they didn't understand her.

The women still did not understand her. They too barked at her and bared their teeth.

She began to bleed and went to the beach to wash off the blood. She stepped into the water.

Occasionally, between one wave and another, a trickle of blood appeared then disappeared.

Anthea's Father

Something clicked in her neck and Anthea went blank. Her mother, sitting in the next room, didn't realize that Anthea had fallen to the floor. Not until the *muzhik* ransom collectors, deployed by the government, came to take the chair in which the mother had been sitting and the one in which Anthea had been sitting before she fell.

Anthea was wearing a long, white gown and had a white peony behind her right ear. For her, white had become the color of mourning and, just before she was felled, she sat gazing through a window grieving the loss of her lover through betrayal. He had joined the *Komsomol* movement when it swept the country, and from his quarters a few miles away he was now directing the *muzhiks* in carrying out their duties.

The poor *muzhiks* were embarrassed to come upon such a pretty sight for the purpose of removing chairs and other pieces of furniture: an Empire-style couch from France, a Shaker-style table and matching chairs from America, a sideboard of no particular style, and a basket in which Anthea had been keeping skeins of wool which she planned to knit a scarf for her father with, for Christmas.

The house they had lived in for years stood on a promontory, jutting high above the Black Sea, near Odessa. From a bird's eye view, as it flew toward it, the house seemed to touch the sea. It had been built by architects at a time when food was already becoming scarce but wine, from Anthea's father's vineyards, was still plentiful and was used as currency. By the time the collectors came, it, too, had become scarce.

Anthea had lived in the big house all her life, in fact she was born there. A *feltcher* woman, the Russian equivalent of a midwife, came to deliver the mother of the baby. The mother was then free to travel all over Europe and America purchasing antiques that, alas, were later requisitioned by the government.

All the while, a wet nurse fed the baby Anthea, so the father formed a particular attachment to the girl, and until the mother's return a next couple of years later, he was the one to attend to all her needs. During this time he let his stewards run the vineyards

Time passed all too quickly, and after eighteen years and not much other young people being available, Althea became rather restive of the sole company of her father. She turned her affections to a handsome youth in a neighboring village. They met in secret; they hugged in impassioned embraces and swore eternal love.

But, a few months later, the youth turned against Anthea and joined the *Komsomol* movement in opposition to what remained of the decadent, bourgeois middle class. However, had it also been her father's perfidious doing to alienate her lover? Anthea would not entertain such a thought, and she was still planning to knit a scarf for her father for Christmas when he mysteriously disappeared.

Eventually the family found out that he had been deported to Siberia. His fate was sealed when he was unable to pay ransom to his government for his freedom, like thousands of such debtors whom he met in the labor camp. There was an irony in the fact that he would have been perfectly capable of paying the ransom from his vineyards, had they not been converted into a collective farm and the meager proceeds had already gone to the government. Meager, because they were now a much less efficient operation than when they were in his hands.

In Siberia there was scarcity of food, wine was unheard of, there was no toilet paper, not to mention paper for writing letters to his wife and to his beloved daughter. The poor man tried to protest these inequities to the authorities, and in their response, that was when Anthea felt a click in her neck from a silent bullet.

The *muzhik* collectors were a strange lot. When they arrived they were amazed and encouraged by the fact that it was possible to fell a young woman to the floor without a sound, and to easily remove her mother from the chair. They proceeded to denude the debtor's premises. Besides taking the furniture, they took the house apart brick by brick, nail by nail, floorboard by floorboard— why not, they might as well while they were at it, any item would be useful at this time of shortages. Not all the loot landed, as it should have, in the government coffers. They left Anthea lying on the bare ground, and her stunned mother lumped on a rock close to where the house had been.

The whole affair would have passed unnoticed, as did many such affairs, but for the fall of the government a couple of years later. Someone discovered Anthea's white gown stained with dried blood. Though her mother was no longer slumping on her chair, her bones were still there.

Anthea's former lover was brought to identify the gown. Yes, he had sometimes seen her wear it, he testified, thus proving, in the investigators' mind, the lovers' passed intimacy. Since he was still a *Komsomol* member and credited with the liquidation of Anthea and her home, the new a government did not kill him but sent him to a labor camp in Siberia, just in case.

Anthea's father was released from his labor camp and allowed to return home, all the way, thousands of miles south back to Odessa. Grief-stricken on finding out that his wife and daughter had been extinct, he jumped from the promontory where the house once stood, straight into the Black Sea. His ghost that would have haunted the previous government's officials began to haunt the new leader who, like his predecessors, was looking for the next generation of debtors, preferably from Chechnya.

Poor Jerusalem

"Bottoms $^{up!}$" Yitzak said to Rifke, his wife. He had just returned from untiringly shuttling between the Ahmeds and the Aarons, the Johnnies and the Suleimans. "Bottoms $^{up!}$" he said, and they m^{a}d^e l^{o}v^e.

For a while everybody could now feel safe and secure, until intransigence welled ^{up}again and
cascaded
     over
        the
             territory. Poor Jerusalem.
At those times bottoms ^{up}were always down. Nobody liked this, least of all Yitzak whose task it was to keep everyone safe and their bottoms^{up}, and to m^{a}k^e l^{o}v^e to Rifke, his wife.

Yitzak was a man of medium height and mediating disposition. He was also an exceedingly honest man. He always wore his toupee, which he donned every morning. This made him particularly sensitive to shifts in the Jerusalem terrain and hence the right man for the job: if the territory became the least bit shaky his toupee was the first thing to slide
            off
           and
           go.
Jerusalem had always been a city of split religions, loyalties and intentions, where every stone sat heavily on the ramparts of history, and in everyone's backyard. Yitzak too had such stones in his front yard. They cobbled down a
d
  e
    c
      l
        i
          n
            e

to the street, and even farther downhill, blocking the main road.

When Rifke washed their clothes and sheets, she too slushed the soapy water down the

d
e
c
l
i
n
e and onto the street.

The water then flowed to the gutter and all the way to the city sewer. Everyone did as Rifke did. It was an event repeated daily in a desperate attempt to focus on and stabilize everyone's life. But any rumble across the territory was likely to disrupt the flow of soapy water which soon became a raging torrent of intransigence, and turned more bottomsdown. By that time, however, Yitzak's toupee had already slid off, and Yitzak himself had been propelled into action—out of his bed and on his way—shuttling between the Ahmeds and the Aarons, between the Johnnies and the Suleimans, untiringly, unceasingly.

His wife Rifke missed him nights.

But on his return, 'bottoms up!,' he'd say, and, after all the love and sweat they made in the hot Jerusalem night, Rifke was happy to wash their clothes and sheets. Until the intransigence welledup and again

c
a
s
c
a
d e
d over the territory.

Poor Jerusalem.

Letters

Marvin the Donor was a millionaire who had never lost his shirt before. But when he reached the top of the mountain he could not find it. It was his favorite shirt, of soft flannel, and it would keep him warm on his trip to the mountains. His wife had patched it a million times. She's been dead five years, and he still missed her. He thought he had recently heard her voice bidding him to visit the mountains that she had left behind to marry him years ago. "…it's time… time to hear the mountain horn echoing between the peaks," he thought he heard her say.

But where was that shirt? He searched through his knapsack. In his frantic attempt to find it, as he rummaged through the knapsack, he looked around in case the shirt had fallen out, he tripped on a stump, lost his footing and slipped down a jagged slope, between trees, and into a clearing. And with him went the knapsack and its contents: sheets of paper, a pen and a telephone directory.

Marvin carried the directory with him everywhere, he would not go anywhere without it. He used it to look at names and addresses of people and then write to them. For the past couple of years he had been spending most of his time on his life-long passion—writing letters. He wrote to people he had never met and from whom he wanted no reply. He would scan the directory until he came across a name that appealed to his fancy and the next moment he was writing a letter to its bearer; it was all one continuous process. He liked writing letters wherever he went, and he now had planned to write one at the top of the mountain

As he tumbled down the mountainside Marvin banged two parts of his body: his head and his right knee.

'Jesus Christ!' he exclaimed when he finally came to a stop. He slowly rose to his feet, hobbled to the nearest bush and relieved himself. He felt lighter, slightly clearer, but he could not remember where was the path that led to the road where he had left his car. He moved a few steps to the left because that's where his unbanged knee carried him. He then stood still, and after a moment or two he bent down and munched on blueberries that spread at his feet. His head felt numb, but when he saw the telephone directory sprawled a few feet away he thought 'I've got to write a letter.' He had had enough of blueberries, and started fumbling in his knapsack for a piece of paper...

*   *   *

They called Marvin 'the Donor' because he had divested himself of most of his funds and had given them to charities. He still had money, but mostly he had time. "Time is what I have the most of," he would tell his friends, "and I can do with it whatever I want." As a widower, now in his early sixties, he had no demands pressing him no matter how exciting they might have been in the past, and he could pursue his favorite occupation: letter writing, longhand. He felt sure, but with regret, that there would soon be no more hand-written letters. High technology would make such slow activity obsolete.

Even as a young man Marvin loved to write letters. He preferred to write them than to receive them. He had good reasons for this. Almost every letter he had ever received was bad news: a reproach, a refusal, a reprimand. When he was in college his mother would ask in each of her letters: "Why don't you write more?" right after she must have received at least three or four of his. She loved his letters passionately. His father, on the other hand, informed him one day: "I will not send you any more pocket money," and then added: "you spend too much of it on postage stamps."

This seemed rather picayune on the part of a man who could well-afford postage money for his son, but Marvin Senior had a clubfoot that had soured his disposition. The foot was heavy, it clunked and clubbed wherever he went, embarrassing him in front of his employees. Besides, he never liked his son's passion for letter writing, he considered it a frivolity. When Marvin heard his father's edict he decided, right then and there, to become a millionaire.

'That's what I'll be,' he thought, 'and I'll never take money from him again.'

Many years later, when Marvin retired and acquired time and money, he resumed writing letters. He wrote to people whom he had never met, who would not ask anything of him, who would not comment on how much stamps cost those days, nor would there be any other reprisals or repercussions, because he would give the recipients no name or address to which they could send a reply.

Marvin's love of writing letters extended to the paraphernalia he used. Since his youth he has been accustomed to the fountain pen. He would carefully choose the nib: not too hard, not too soft. The color of the ink would always be black, this he never varied. Black, he felt, was the most elegant, the most forceful and unambiguous of colors. As much as he loved writing letters, Marvin had not been able to indulge in it fully until after his wife's death. Not that she had been demanding of his time, but while she was alive he somehow lacked the emotional impetus to do it, weighed down as he was by his attachment to her. Her passing released him enough to begin writing.

He had yet to decide how he would find recipients for his letters. He had no clear idea how to begin, where to send his letters, yet he felt confident that after a few nights' good sleep something would transpire. From past experience he knew that an idea takes time to incubate in the subterranean regions of the mind, 'but when it is ripe,' Marvin thought, 'a good night's sleep is all that's needed.' And when it came he had to be ready with paper, ink, etc.

He went to a stationary store in town that sold letter sheets by the pound, in various colors and shades, with matching envelopes, all recycled paper. From sunny yellow to mellow creamy, from dark mauve to light orchid. There were off-whites and pale grays with wispy specks giving the paper a slightly textured look. He marveled at the selection, admired the shades and colors, and, considering the amount of writing he planned to do, he knew that in time he would use all those varieties. Grays and blues, for example, would be for men, pinks and orchids for women; shades of green might be for people who had some kind of verdure in their address.

Marvin bought a few pounds of assorted sheets and envelopes, and hurried home. It was early autumn and, after summer's outwardly activities, Marvin felt ready to turn inward and start writing. One morning, after a good night's sleep, as he was wondering how he would go about finding people to whom he would address his letters, his eyes fell on a telephone directory.

When Marvin was growing up, there were always old telephone directories lying about his parents' home. His mother never threw them away. Like so many other things, she found them delectable, not that she would eat them, no—chocolate was her only edible indulgence—but as things she could possess, hoard, accumulate. Some directories, where she had scribbled and underlined names, pre-dated her marriage. She had kept them for fear of giving up her girlhood, and she used them to keep track of the people she had known in her youth. By the time Marvin was born and of reading age, some of them had yellowed, the pages tattered here and there, corners bent, a few accidentally torn off. They acquired an aura of antiquity to such a degree that even his father, who ran a tight and tidy ship but was fond of antiques, accepted them in the house and let them lie about.

As a boy, Marvin spent many hours perusing the directories as one might peruse the pages of an encyclopedia. What he learned was not knowledge but the extent to which his imagination could be stirred. He memorized names and addresses that had a visual, gustatory, auditory, olfactory, even an emotional appeal. Names like Cherry, or Butter, or Green, Rose, Spur, Sprint or Spittle would send him into transports. He would delight in all the Plum Coves, and Brier Lanes and Birch Roads. He would repeat them at odd moments, at the dinner table, or while dressing for school in the morning, or he would sing them in the shower. Singing in the shower was something his father never did, he was not that kind of a man, and therefore Marvin's habit of singing names and addresses at such moments was to his father a source of constant irritation. But, as the boy grew, this habit etched in his memory-cortex a facility for remembering names like someone who early in life acquires a facility for languages; this facility stood him in good stead later, when the demands of his career called upon it. And by the same token it finally exonerated him in his father's eyes, because it allowed Marvin to become a millionaire.

That early autumn morning when he was finally ready to begin writing, Marvin looked at his telephone directory. He had scarcely used it, preferring to call 411 and hear a human voice, especially since his wife's death. But now, no human hand or voice could accomplish what he needed to do himself. He looked at his hands and spread his fingers wide. His joints were slightly thickened with arthritis, 'but these fingers can still do the walking,' he thought, quoting the Yellow Pages, 'and find recipients of my letters. I'll use the telephone directory, that's what I'll do.'

But first breakfast—cold cereal and orange juice. He has not had a hot breakfast since his wife's passing. She had brought her cooking habits into the marriage, there was always hot breakfast in her home in the cool mountains where she came from. Marvin then changed the shirt he had slipped on earlier to his favorite one of soft flannel with checkered design: moss-green, cherry-red and black. He was truly fond of this shirt. It gave him solace and comfort and wrapped around him like an outsize cuddly teddy bear. It had cost him one dollar at a Salvation Army store where he bought his clothes before he became a millionaire. After he married, his wife would carefully mend any hole that appeared in it. She would match the moss-green, cherry-red and black threads and weave them in a tight and tidy crisscross fashion until the hole was filled to her satisfaction.

New holes had by now appeared in the old shirt, yet he would not trust anyone to match the colors of the threads and weave them as well as his wife had done. 'Maybe it's time to throw the shirt away' he wondered. But trash-day after trash-day came and went, and he could not bring himself to do it. So he wrapped himself in the shirt, and sat down to write his first letter.

Flipping through the first few pages of the telephone directory—'Emergency', 'Consumer Guide', 'How to reach us at...', 'Self Help Guide', etc., etc., he came to the first page of names. There was Abbott S. He liked the name. It reminded him of eminences in their loose and graceful robes, flitting through the shaded courtyards and abbeys he had seen in Europe. He looked through the colored sheets of paper. Mauve, he thought, would be the right color for an ecclesiastical name like Abbott, and he pulled out a mauve-colored sheet; a green envelope would be for the verdure in Abbott's address. And almost without a moment's hesitation, as if finding the name had instantaneously released a flow of ideas, he began:

Dear Abbott,

 I am wondering what it is like to be the first person in a telephone directory, he wrote in his smooth, cursive style. I have been first in many things, but not in a telephone directory, so being first here seems rather charming. At first glance you are just a name, but a name that suggests deep-rooted ecclesiastical connections. Have you ever thought of that, have you had any, ever used them? If you were an abbot you would be the first-ranked person in an abbey.

 But oh, forgive me—I have not given you my reasons for writing this letter. Rest assured that I am not writing for any favors, a reciprocation, for forgiveness of my sins, or—perish the thought!— for a donation. All this you may expect from family, friends or charities, but not from me, an anonym. Wait! Do not let this letter go the way of most anonymous letters, to your waste paper basket. Read on. I do not presume to give advice, only a recommendation, a rather personal one, to which you will come if you read on. But, dear Abbott, let me just wonder for one more moment—are you the first, not only in the directory, but also in someone's consideration?

If you are not, this letter may have a bearing on what you could do with your life henceforward.

I notice (and pardon yet another digression), that you live on Barberry Lane, Marvin went on after adjusting the the cushion that propped up his back, and mulling over the address after the name.

Let me suggest that you would be sorely amiss not to notice and reflect deeply upon the name of your street along the following lines: first, I do hope that the thorny barberry shrubs are there, aren't they? If they are not, maybe you ought to plant them, but avoid brushing against them lest they give you pain.
Secondly, consider the berries which, when red and ripe, must look beautiful as they dangle from the bushes along your lane. I understand they are sour, but are they edible? I myself like sour fruit, especially sour cherries which are very difficult to find unless you are in the jam-making business, which I am not. In fact, I have divested myself of all business.

And here I come to the most serious point of my letter: not presuming to give advice, I suggest that you do everything possible to set yourself free, as I have done, and let letter writing become your main preoccupation. You may already have waited too long, and have no one to write to. In that case pick up a telephone directory, and choose the first person your eye or finger alights upon. Do not start from the beginning of the directory as I have done, or you will find yourself writing to yourself. Try 'B's' or 'D's', look under 'Z's'—there are some fascinating names there, although these are less intelligible to the English mind. In any case, in the process of writing a letter you will, I suspect, begin to place all your concerns, hopes, wishes, prejudices on the person to whom you are writing and, in time, if you're not careful, you will, I'm warning you, find yourself no longer free, but as attached, hence encumbered, as you have ever been.

Therefore, dear Abbott, here Marvin's hand paused for a moment, I must heed my own warning, and quickly end this letter lest that dreaded thing happens to me.

With all due regards,

Yours.

In the In the next several months Marvin wrote many letters, playing with names, addresses, colors of paper, but always quick to avoid that dreaded thing—encumbrance. Yet one encumbrance, especially from his own past, such as his father's clubfoot he could not avoid. When he came to the name 'Foote R' his spirit, much stepped upon in his youth, sought expression. And so Marvin wrote to the unsuspecting Mr. Foote.

Dear Mr. Foote,

... some parts of the body, he wrote, are destined for idioms: 'arm's length,' 'to have a nose for something,' etc., and the foot is no exception. But I hope, Mr. Foote, that your life, unlike mine, has not been affected by the foot (my dictionary of idioms indicates that it could have been in thirty-seven different ways) to any greater extent than footing bills. I hope that you have not gotten off on the wrong foot with anyone, as I had so often done with my father, even though that experience taught me early on to stand on my own two feet.

If I were to share with you, which I'll refrain from doing, some information about my father's medical condition, you would understand my preoccupation with the foot. Yet, since my eye caught your name in the telephone directory, I do want to tell you some of my thoughts about the foot.

Here Marvin wondered whether he had chosen the right color for his letter to Foote R, namely dusky buff. It was the color of the shoe his father wore on his clubfoot. It fit the color of feet that had not been washed too often, but would it fit the pearly hue of clean, well-tended feet? Yet it was a color that suited the seriousness of the subject matter, Marvin thought. There was an added consideration: Mr. Foote's choice to live on Oxford Road implied a bookish nature which harmonized well with the somber color of dusky buff.

Marvin picked up his pen again.

Have you ever thought, Mr. Foote, he wrote, of the foot that presses the pedal of a motor vehicle: of a truck that dashes about, of a sedan that cruises sedately, of a black or red Corvette that zooms past you like a race car? They all have a foot pressing on a pedal. It could be a foot that has stepped out of a shower that morning and is sheathed in a clean, silk sock, or a foot that has not been near water for days and days, a cheesy, smelly foot, or kicked a ball on a playing field, or a foot that has just come back from a hike along a dusty path in the mountains.

There was more to follow, but Marvin felt he owed Foote an apology for writing him such a long letter.

I am truly indebted to you, Mr. Foote, for the name you carry, Marvin went on. It gives me a chance to express my thoughts, long buried, about the foot. But please understand that you are under no obligation to continue reading this letter, and I apologize if it has caused you any discomfort.

Yet I am asking you to dwell on the foot, the one pressing on the pedal, a while longer, because, in my travels down the highways, I tend to dwell on it quite a bit: it is either a foot which has been carefully pedicured and powdered with perfumed talcum powder, or one that constantly battles the nuisance of 'athlete's foot' and is dusted with something that is no more fun than Desenex powder. Yet either foot presses the pedal with more or less efficiency, less when it ends in a crash, more when it arrives home safely.

The foot, Mr. Foote, which has the most appeal to me, is the foot that is pressing the pedal on its way to and from ballet lessons. It is not always perfectly clean, especially on its way home from a ballet lesson, sweaty, with particles of coalesced dust between its toes, but it is strong, and, didn't I already mention a pearly hue? Yes, it has a pearly hue accentuated by purplish veins; what's more, it has become (after prolonged and strenuous training) perfectly adapted to carrying in a most unnatural position—the weight of a human body.

You may wonder, Mr. Foote, what has inspired my interest in the ballet foot. It is my darling sister's pearly-hued feet, driven by my mother to and from ballet lessons, until my sister (a tall, winsome girl with the complexion of a camellia, as I remember her from our youth) was old enough to push that pedal with her own foot.

But time has come, dear Mr. Foote, to end this letter, because I feel that I have at last gotten the foot off my chest, the foot that has rankled me all my life, has been pressing on me all these years and has driven me to places I would rather not have gone (was this something I should have confessed to the Abbott?).

I cannot totally blame my father for it, he was not all bad. It was just his foot. His other parts were fine: he had a hand in my education, an eye for antiques, and his heart was in the right place.

I therefore I want to leave you, Mr. Foote, on the final note that there is more to life than the foot.

Yours ever.

Another day, while searching through the directory in alphabetical order, Marvin came upon a curious thing. The name Grieco, with its phonetic association with El Greco was fascinating enough. But the curious thing was the double listing of the same name at the same address spelled in two different ways: Gap Head Rd and Gaphead Rd. What gave the address its eerie quality were of course the 'gap' and the 'head'. Was the gap an opening made by breaking of or parting on the head, Marvin wondered, or was it a mountain pass, a ravine, or maybe a blank space, a lag, a disparity? Did the head refer to the part of the body which contains the brain, or was it the head on a nail, the froth on a pint of ale, or a toilet on a boat? Marvin decided to write to the addressee, and although he would not obtain a reply, he hoped to find his own answer in the process.

Dear Grieco, he wrote, do you realize where you live? Pardon my temerity, but this is a most serious matter requiring your immediate attention. Do you live at a gap on a human head, or at a gap (no, tha's impossible!) between a pint and its frothy head? Or do you live at the head of a mountain pass, a ravine, or at the head of a land that has been split in two? Is there a space, a lag or a disparity where you live, and if so, in whose head? Maybe in the head of the typesetter who, in his anxiety about the street name, spelled it in two different ways.

Here Marvin stopped and wondered whether, regardless of his own sense of urgency, he should send the letter at all. He went on wondering about heads, about gaps in his own head; he went on marveling at the name of the street. He savored it and mulled it over until, sadly, he came to the conclusion that he was the gaphead. He let his imagination roam over the expanses of his psyche, and left the letter unfinished, unmailed.

One day the listing 'Flickinger F & G Gee Ave' caught Marvin in an unusually flippant mood.

Dear Flick-in-ger, he wrote, *with the flick of a finger, that's all it took, I found you in the big book, my venue for self-expression— the telephone directory. And you live on Gee Ave, gee whiz! This must be one of my up days, so I take to paper post haste. Not much sense here, but my already buoyant spirit is buoying even higher. Sense isn't everything, spirit counts for more, especially when it's the beautifully advertised 'Absolut'! So gee, thanks for being there, stay there, and don't move for at least a few more annual issues of the directory.*
     Yours.

Days wore on from dawn to dusk, outer events being as un-varied as his inner ones were multifarious. Marvin still missed his wife. It has been a long time since he had sex, or written a love letter to her or to anyone else. He looked long and hard through the telephone directory for a name that would reflect his mood.

Bragdon D ...... no.
Caggiano S ...... no.
etc., etc., ... no.

He found very few women's names listed alone. They were mostly joined with a man's name. Finally his eyes caught: Camille O. Reynard Ct., 'oh, what a name!' he thought, 'must be a woman's, and living on Reynard Court! In French *renard*... a fox... fox the mystifier... that's you, my first love!'

Marvin looked through the colored sheets of his writing paper, and finally chose mallow pink. He had seen mallows bloom in country gardens, each one tall, upright and soft like a woman. He always liked tall women, like his sister. And anytime he passed a tall woman in the street he imagined her with a huge belly, pregnant. He would see her in his mind, spreading her strong thighs to give birth.

Oh, Camille, Camille, he finally began his letter, why did you leave me at a time when the best was yet to come, when mallows were still in bloom, and your overgrown body needed nourishment with love, not with multivitamins? I still see you leaning over your garden fence and remember how rooted I thought you were. Not in dirt or manure (like mallows), but in the quixos and quaxos of everyday love. I see you sitting on a kitchen stool peeling potatoes for the two of us, while in my ears trumpets of love are blaring. I see you pick up and mend my underpants while through my veins the Gulf Stream is rushing.

But then... you began looking at other men, and a knife went through my rib-cage. To mollify its effect I would pick up my worry-stone (so as not to worry you) and rub it with my thumb into my palm till I believed that there appeared an indentation that I had actually made. You would come to me and smile. I knew that smile, and I still know it whenever I see it on a woman's face: it is the smile of fox the mystifier.

'Where are the dews of yesteryear?' Marvin mused and wondered if he should continue the letter, if he should send it to Camille O. Long gone were the days of the worry-stone, long gone were the days of mallows rooted in dirt and manure, long gone were the days of thighs spread wide to give birth to a child.

And his wife was dead now. Long gone seemed the days of the weaving the threads, moss-green, cherry-red and black, long gone was her soul's wearying and worrying that she would never see the mountains she had left to marry him, the mountains where she had listened to the echo of a song blown on a shepherd's horn many miles away… She had often talked about it, but they never went to listen to it. They just went on living, he believing her about the echo, she longing for it.

Another summer was gliding by and glistening with moist and slippery grass, blueberry bushes were bearing fruit. Marvin seemed less energetic, he wrote fewer letters, but if he ever left the house he still brought with him his pen, a few sheets of paper and his telephone directory, just in case. He dwelt a lot on memories of his wife and thought he heard her voice: once in the cupboard when he looked for a cup to fill with instant coffee, once when he opened a closet in search of a clean towel, once when he lifted the bed covers to shake them a bit and throw them back on the bed. "It's time… time to hear the echo in the mountains…" he thought he heard her call.

He rummaged through a closet full of crumpled stuff that he had not used in years and found an old knapsack. He packed a sweater and, he thought, his checkered flannel shirt, he packed his telephone directory, a few sheets of writing paper, his pen, and he set off for the mountains.

…His head hurt from the bang he sustained while slipping and sliding down the jagged mountain slope. He had had enough of blueberries and was now fumbling in his knapsack for a piece of paper, white this time, because he had not chosen anyone to write to before he left home. He would copy the letter onto an

appropriately colored sheet when he returned home… home…
He reached for the directory that had fallen out of the knapsack,
sprawled nearby on the ground. It seemed heavier than usual. He
opened it somewhere in the middle, tried to pick out a name, but
the print was fuzzy…

Yet the air was clear and, far in the distance, he heard a sound.
But, unbeknownst to him, the pia and the dura mater, the two
delicate sheaths of tissue enveloping his brain were gradually
separating from one another due to a slow seepage of blood from
a torn vein, the blood now clotting and forming a blob, pressing
on his brain. Yet he still heard the sound and, with the last flicker
of awareness, he realized it was the echo of a mountain horn
blowing far away.

Fawning

Elephant heads and rumps are locked into rounded boulders, boulders with folds and creases like elephant skin. Gnomes move in to guard the elephants. Cracks in the boulders are their smiles, not yet obsequious like sycophants', but wait a while. They slowly uncover the boulders, brush off the dirt and look, but uncover no treasures. Not yet. On any given day they dig the dirt, and brush it off just enough to show more elephant skin.

They go on digging the dirt and show more stone, more boulders with folds and creases like elephant skin. They smile as they do their digging. But slowly their smiles that were the cracks and creases in the boulders like elephant skin, turn obsequious like sycophants'.

We'll just go on digging the dirt, say the gnomes, we'll move the dirt out to sea on barges in rounded heaps. We'll dig the dirt, but we need sycophants to do dirt to the elephants.

Yes, say the sycophants, but we first need some gallants to fawn them for permission to do the dirt.

No one will know the difference, permission or no permission, so say the gnomes, and smile obsequiously at the cracks in the boulders like creases in elephant skin.

Oh yes, someone will know the difference, but it's still much too early, too early in the morning to do dirt, say the sycophants, the fog has not yet burnt off. And it's too early for fawning. It's still rush-hour gridlock, they say, twiddling their steering wheels in this rush-hour morning.

They finally find some gallants to fawn for permission before they've had their first cup of coffee. No, no, it's too early, the gallants say, let us wait till dusk.

No, no, say the gnomes, why wait till dusk? From morning till dusk is too long to wait, it's too late to dig and do dirt at dusk. Let us start at a decent hour.

We need our first cup of coffee first, the sycophants say, to fawn the gallants.

Then let's make it right after, the gnomes concede, then you'll fawn the gallants this morning. We'll bring jukeboxes, put in some dimes and set them blaring into the air. And into the air we'll belt out guffaws and belt out our songs. No one will know the difference between us gnomes, sycophants, and elephant heads—except the elephants. We'll dig out their tusks out of the dirt, they'll bring in so much money, oh, so much money.

Early next morning and right after the first cup of coffee, the gridlock blaring and honking, the jukeboxes belting out songs, the gallants' heads, having arrived are also bobbing to the tune, the gnomes go on smiling, as the sycophants will do their fawning to let them do dirt to the elephants.

What a thing to happen first thing, say the gallants, right after the first cup of coffee in the morning! We thought the gnomes were guarding those tusks. The gallants go bobbing their heads in the morning.

Oh, but they do guard, they do, say the sycophants, we're the ones doing dirt, not the gnomes. Just give us permission to do in the elephants, their tusks will bring in so much money, oh, so much money.

But the gnomes will never let you, say the gallant heads, they guard the elephants grounded in the boulders, so quit it, quit your fawning.

The sycophants nudge each other. But, yes they'll let us, they will, they've already started removing heaps of dirt to the barges and out to sea earlier this morning.

Why all the fuss, then? Quit your fawning and start doing dirt to the elephants, says first one gallant head. And soon another head nods, then another, till all the gallant heads are nodding and bobbing.

The boulders moved, more dirt dug away, the jukeboxes blaring guffaws into the air, now one gallant after another no longer knowing the difference between gnomes, elephant heads and sycophants. No difference either, between one gallant head bobbing and another. One guffaw after another, the bobbing gallant heads watch the gnomes dig dirt and the sycophants do dirt to the elephants.

And all through the morning and the entire day the jukeboxes blare.

Then suddenly at dusk, one jukebox, oh, so sweetly and discretely cranks out a different song. And, just then, at dusk, suddenly one gallant head goes bobbing on an elephant's tusk. Bobbing and bouncing. And as the tune tinkles on, oh, so sweetly and discretely, first a gnome, then a sycophant goes dangling from another elephant's tusks. Then more and more and well beyond dusk, more gallant heads, gnomes, and sycophants go dangling, bobbing and bouncing on elephants' tusks, the elephants meanwhile dancing. And well beyond dusk the jukebox sings—oh, so sweetly and discretely, in tunes melting round the elephants' ears. The dirt gone to sea on barges, the elephants now walk to a meadow, and over a whippoorwill's whoop and into the night of juicy berry bushes, the elephants go dancing and dancing well into dawn and beyond, to a lark's silvery song.

Words—a Whimsy

Not finding words for beauty? Go to a meadow.
Not finding words for cleanliness? Go to a laundromat.
Not finding words for fear? Go to your bank.

She went to a meadow, wearing a linen blouse she had just bought. There was a shush of gentle breeze, blue cornflowers accented the softness of clouds of grasses, some stray flax seeds sprouted, a skylark hovered above in song. Were these the words she needed?

Some distance away, there was a man lying on the grass, not too far so she could see his blond hair; he was reclining against the stump of a tree that must have been felled long ago. Was he the one she met first, his gray eyes saddened by what he knew, or the one she danced with later, their bodies tightly following the rhythm and no words said, or now, much later still, this man here in the meadow? Are these the right words?

She went to a laundromat, looking for the word for cleanliness. The machines were white and shiny, turning at a steady pace, not a spec of dirt on the floor—was this it, the words she needed? He too was there, now it seemed emanating sensuality. Must have noticed her somewhere. He showed her how to wash and fold.

She went to a bank in her hometown by the sea. The upholstered sofas, the dark wood paneling and counters, their opulence scared her. Were these the words of fear? Not quite.

Suddenly the door opened and he, the same man, entered the bank. She blushed. He was in a naval uniform, stripes on his sleeves. Now truly scared of his soon to supervise casting off his ship's ropes, she was about to leave. He approached her and gently took her hand, brought it to his lips and kissed it. He then led her out to the street, slowly, no words spoken until they reached the wharf.

"Wait for me," he then said, "I will be back."

These were his only words. As he stepped onto the gangplank, then onto the ship's deck, tears began to flow down her cheeks. She had no hankie, so they flowed onto her chest and dried off on the linen of her blouse. She had bought the blouse somewhere long ago. No, she bought it recently at a local store, on her way to the meadow, looking for words.

Obsession Run Riot

The water was swishing at the seashore not back and forth but like a river flowing. Much was to be gained by this anomaly. It was something we couldn't understand, but we were only children at the time.

Betty was already in bed, and I was on the last button of my pajamas. I closed the window of our bedroom to shut out the swishing of the ocean. But the door was still open and I tried to listen to Mother's and her sister Auntie's conversation. The more I heard the more I suspected that Auntie would eventually play us a trick.

"Tululah has gone mad," Auntie was saying, "and that's why her house blew up and was swished into the sea."

"How do you know this?" Mother asked.

"By divination."

"By what?"

"Divination."

That's all I heard and I didn't I understand the word, so I didn't bother listening anymore and I closed the door. I decided to look up the word next morning, finished buttoning my p.j.'s and went to sleep.

Mother knew the meaning, I was sure, but she didn't tell us. She was too busy taking care of us, but I also had a feeling that this was her way of keeping us in the dark. Of course Tululah couldn't tell us anything because she was gone with her house. The secret lay with Auntie and with Mother, but neither of them would tell us what it was all about. In the meantime, we had to attend school, do our homework, the dishes after dinner, so we didn't have any spare time. But time was of the essence because Tululah's house had been by the seashore and, as I had mentioned, the water was swishing in a continuous flow like river, washing everything away, not leaving much for any investigation.

As we grew older, any one of us, aware of Auntie's strangeness, should have figured this out.

While I was recalling those days years later, I was struck by the confusion of it all. And yet, there must have been a thread tying it all together—perhaps Auntie's "divination."

At that time Tululah and Auntie had been great friends and almost inseparable since their high school days, even more so than Betty and I had been as kids. They went to the same community college, not being a material for higher education, and shared their dorm room. Auntie went so far as fluff up Tululah's pillow and tuck her in at bed time. She even tried to spoon-feed her after she brought something special for her from the student cafeteria. As she was telling us this, young as I was, I found it odd how Tululah could have taken it all. After graduating they both returned home to our town. I remember a smirk on my mother's face when she would ask Auntie to go to the movies with her.

"Wait," Auntie would say, "I have to ask Tululah, in case she had already made plans for the two of us."

This went on for a few years, but then something changed. Occasionally, Tululah didn't answer her phone, Auntie complained. When questioned later, she would tell Auntie that she had a terrible headache and couldn't get to the phone fast enough. After a few such times Auntie became suspicious. Once, when she ran into Tululah's cleaning woman downtown and asked her about Tululah's headaches when she was cleaning her house that day, "you know what she said? That Miss Tululah wasn't home!"

Spring and early summer were beautiful that year. The garden acacia was blooming earlier than usual and its aroma in our back yard surpassed the fragrance of my French perfumes. Sunlight and frequent showers made our lawn more lush than ever before. Everyone was taking walks during their lunch time. Even our mayor was back late for his office hours, as he was stopping to smell people's front yards.

One such time he ran into young Harry from his office, Betty told me, and she overheard their conversation.

"How is it going, m' boy?" the mayor asked.

"Very well, sir," Harry answered.

"Well, well, m' boy, tell me more."

"It's a secret, but some people seem to know."

"Then I should know too."

"Tululah and I are getting closer by the day, sir."

Betty didn't tell this to anybody except us, but the way secrets travel on air, in innuendoes, on "I'll tell you but keep it to yourself" conversations, they may as well not be secrets. And that's how it came to Auntie's ears. She didn't blow up but she made a plan that she later carried out.

After the beautiful spring, summer and fall, when winter came it was severe. Houses built along the shore were one by one pulled into the sea by the heavy storms.

One of them was Tutulah's. What happened before that was anybody's guess, but all along, as we found out much later, and blood being thicker than water, Mother had kept secret what Auntie had told her behind our closed bedroom door, including the meaning of her sister's strange word—"divination." Yet, a couple of years before Mother died, to relieve her guilt of not having done anything about it, she finally told us how Auntie had described her plan.

One afternoon Auntie invited Tululah for coffee at her house. She baked delicious little cakes for her, and as they sat drinking coffee and appreciating the early sunset, Mother remembered the rest of their conversation as Auntie related it to her almost verbatim: "… one of these cold and dreary evenings, why don't you line up some candles by your windows, lay them on their sides, wick to wick, and light them up?" Auntie told her.

"But why should I do it this way?" Tululah asked.

"To produce a more continuous effect."

"Great idea!"

"Let me know what day you want to do it. I'll get the candles, come to you house, and I'll help you set them up."

On the appointed day, Auntie arrived at Tululah's house with the candles, a sheet of plastic, and a small parcel of something with a string attached to it. Then more of what was said:

"What's that?" Tululah asked.

"Just a jar of cookies you might enjoy later."

"And the plastic?"

"After we've laid the candles wick to wick and you're going to light them some night, the plastic is to prevent the wax from dripping all over your windowsills."

"And the string attached to one of the candles, what that's for?"

"Just to steady the candles."

Auntie helped Tululah set up the candles, she told Mother, and as she was leaving she dropped the small parcel, with the string attached, inside the front door.

A particularly stormy night was being predicted for the following night, Mother said. Tululah must have thought this would be a particularly good time to light the candles for people to be cheered by their light. As the evening darkened, Tululah proceeded to do what Auntie had suggested.

Everyone in the vicinity and beyond were horrified to see Tululah's house blow up and slide into the ocean with Tululah inside it.

Horrific as this was, Mother told us, no one had time or energy to investigate why Tululah's house had been blown up. Those close to the shore were perplexed why the swishing of the waters went in one direction instead of back and forth. Some of the houses had been blown up by the impact of the waters. They fell apart during the storms, the reason being that they were old and had not been built to code. Their owners were relieved by the swishing of the waters in one direction because the cause of the disappearance of their houses could not be ascertained, and they received compensation, no questions asked. Nonetheless the wrangling and court procedures took months.

And so it went until the following spring, when one day, Mother said, kids playing by the shore where Tululah's house had been found a rusty can, singed at its rim. But Auntie was dead by then due to a heart attack, and the meaning of her word "divination" had long been swished away into the sea.

Each Time It Rained

It had nothing to do with the rain. They've gone through rains before, heavy rains, thunder and lightning. But now, each time it poured, all neighbors, except a local roofer, would congregate under a roof, the same roof as always, over the big room and beg forgiveness.

The roof had been repaired many times, but there was one corner in the top room where it still leaked. First dampness appeared, then a mold began to grow, and each time it leaked, the mold along the adjoining wall grew bigger.

The owners of the house, in their absence, and because they had other things on their minds, were not aware of what was happening.

That's how the story, told much later, unraveled. It spread from one person to another, in details ever more complex. In retrospect, some people were confused and wanted to draw a causal relationship between the events and the mold, but they later realized that making such a connection would have been sheer nonsense.

A little girl, whom they all knew as Tilly, was found strangled in the owners' top room, with bent willow twigs that looked like a necklace. It had been her parents' bedroom, which later became almost a sanctuary to the memory of the dead child.

Her parents were implicated at first, partially because there was no love lost between them and the neighboring community. Her father had never needed to work long hours, for minimum wage, at some McDonald's. Her mother had never needed to wash anyone's floors, not even her own, because they had a maid from across the border in their employ.

Tilly had a roof over her head and food in her stomach but not much else. Her parents were either away on business or traveling for pleasure.

It looked like the child had not been born to a family, or to the community, or to any village or town. She was born onto herself: she lived, and played mostly by herself, occasionally with the maid. But no mother in the community ever suggested that once in a while she come play with her kids. No father expressed concern if she was adequately supervised, playing alone by a nearby stream.

At Tilly's pleading, the maid would take her on long drives, along the surrounding green fields, oak groves and rows of willow trees along the stream. Tilly liked, it seemed, to visit the willow trees the best. Their long strands reaching down to the water may have reminded her of her own wispy hair that the maid would comb every morning. She was pretty, but not as pretty as Jon Benet, whose photo clippings lay around from her parents' old magazines.

The old people in town remembered the tragedy, and everyone worried that Tilly's fate would follow suit.

The investigators were very thorough. Fingerprints on Tilly's body didn't point to anyone around. The necklace puzzled them, and when they found out her fondness for willow trees, the maid became a suspect. The child was known to play with a necklace that the maid had shown her how to make out of willow twigs. But the maid's fingerprints were not on the necklace of the strangling object.

Eventually the parents' innocence was established because they were away at the time of the murder, and they let the maid return to her people in Laredo. They continued to spend a lot of time away from home because of bad memories.

At first the only question, unasked and unanswered, was about the roofing company, a local outfit. In an unrelated event sometime before Tilly's murder, one of their employees, a roofer, went berserk and was admitted to a local mental hospital. When questioned at an interview, he said he had been stewing about his low wages for a long time. No one had noticed his bad mood or approached him when he seemed dismal. Finally, when he was threatened with dismissal for his ill temper, he snapped, the simmering symptoms of his long-standing illness were unleashed and he was hospitalized. After a brief stay in the hospital, he was transferred for follow-up and care to a local facility.

Granted, the unfortunate roofer received some attention, but who really knew about his comings and goings out of the facility? Or about his unresolved grievance toward the roofing company. He had no chance to talk to a psychotherapist, because he had none. None was available or they did not assign him one. He would have confided that he still felt his roofing company needed to learn a lesson and pay for it.

However, he did have an occupational therapist at the care center, who had all kinds of gadgets and materials in her assigned room for his diversion: for weaving baskets and sewing on buttons, there were cooking utensils so he could occasionally make a dessert to try make contact with his housemates.

He was particularly fascinated by the strands of willow twigs that the therapist brought for weaving various kinds of arty objects, especially in early spring just after the sap rose and when they had first year branches. They bent and peeled easily, and were used for making small bracelets and necklaces.

He remembered the willow trees that grew on the outskirts of his town. Before his breakdown, he would sometimes stop to look at them on his way to work. Occasionally, he saw a little girl there, playing alone, and a young woman watching her at a distance, immersed in reading a book. He would turn down his window and listen to the child's laughter as she was taking hold of the bigger branches and swing over the stream. A good chance to abduct the girl, but he was not that kind of a man. Instead, he thought wouldn't it be nice to weave a little necklace with the willow twigs and bring it to the little girl, who he thought might need some cheering up.

He now followed instructions how to make a small necklace, then got permission to take the bus to his hometown for a few hours.

Sometime later the occupational therapist, who in her wildest or not so wild imagination could not connect willow twigs to anything evil, finally heard about Tilly's death and the necklace. The full story began to unravel and ended at an inquest.

The roofer had a public defender but he asked to speak for himself. At this time he was considered competent to stand trial and was allowed his request. They first called the occupational therapist to testify.

"What did you think of the defendant?" the state prosecutor asked.

"He was so nice. Not very bright, but he was our best weaver, so meticulous in every detail," she replied.

"Did you sense any nastiness?"

"No, your honor."

They called the roofer next.

"Tell us what happened," asked the prosecutor.

"I thought the little girl ma't need some cheerin' up and would enjoy a necklace I'd made for her at my care center."

"So what happened next?" the prosecutor pressed on.

"When I got to the house, the girl was alone at the door, the maid must've gone shoppin.'"

"And then?"

"She looked so nice and soft. I thought she'd like the necklace I showed her but for some reason, I don't know why, the girl got uneasy, then scared, and ran all the way up to the top room. I followed her and tried to put the necklace over her little head."

"And then what happened?" The roofer's defender asked for permission to testify. He knew what had happened but didn't want to scare the roofer from telling his story.

"She tried to shove me off, so I got annoyed and tried to force the darn thing down 'er neck."

A chill went through the court.

"And?"

"The necklace must have got tightened somehow from her neck swellin' or somethin' and the girl swooned."

"So what did you do?" asked the prosecutor.

"I didn't think much of it, figured she'd come to, notice the necklace and be happy wit' it. So I made my way down through the house, onto the bus and back to my care center."

The roofer was charged with murder—later commuted to involuntary manslaughter—for having left the child, as she lay there, merely swooned as he had thought. He was released from the court and escorted back to his care center.

After a couple of months, the roofer's mental condition stabilized, and he was discharged from the center to return to the town and the place where he had lived before the tragedy.

Unemployed, unoccupied, though occasionally reporting to his probation officer, he had plenty of time to think, mainly about his former roofing company. He remembered what the occupational therapist had said about second-year willow twigs being stronger and used for making baskets. He also remembered that when he was working for the roofing company, he had noticed a small crack in the roof right over the big bedroom, which no one else saw, and which could have caused the dampness inside. He felt this was none of his business but of the owners' and of the company's inspectors.

He was a hefty fellow, though bow-legged, because when he was little his mother didn't have enough milk to feed him. He lacked calcium and grew soft bones that eventually bent under his increasing weight. His mother was a good woman and tried to take good care of him. But not his father, who wanted to be sure his wife served him steak and eggs for breakfast and not so sure if there was enough milk in the fridge for his little boy. He spent more time fishing with guys than with his son, and fixing his pick-up truck so it could stand the mud-race in the next village fair.

When the boy grew up, bow-legged as he was, he was nimble and tolerated heights well enough to train as a roofer. However, the company that hired him did not treat their workers well, and the roofer was particularly sensitive. His hostility about their neglect of his needs mounted. Their threat to fire him finally led to his break down.

A couple of months after discharge from the care center, remembering the hard second-year twigs gave him an idea. He began to collect them. Unnoticed by anyone, he went on with his plan to bring the company had worked for to justice. Climbing the roof of the big house at night and every night, and one push after another with his twigs, occasional rain and drizzle softening the passage, he extended the crack he knew had been there, until he felt a weakening resistance and figured he must have reached with his twigs close to the inside the wall of the big room. He stopped and waited.

About three or four weeks elapsed and he thought this was enough time for mold to appear.

When the owners returned after their long absence, he heard a lot of noise around the house and wondered what the fuss was all about. Then, the one word he began to hear downtown was *mold, mold*. The owners tried to reach the roofing company, but found out it was no longer there. They hired another company, and that's when the hard willow twigs, extending from the roof to the big room were discovered and the damage repaired.

By then everyone was worn out by all the events of the preceding months and had no inclination to try find out who, where, when and how it happened. All they could do was to deal with their grief.

And so each time it poured, all the neighbors, except for the roofer, would gather by the side of the house, under that one roof, the same roof as always, and beg forgiveness. Because they knew that the child had not been born to her family but she had been as good as born to their community, to their village and town.

115

Dent-de-Lion

It was small wonder that Joergen grew so pale-green and tall. He was like a plant low on chlorophyll and straining toward sunlight. He lived in the regions of eternal summer sun, but its rays were sparse and of little consequence to Joergen's needs. The few that touched his head with some effectiveness lightened his hair to the color of straw, but they reached to the level of the organ that was his heart only rarely.

The sound of birds that never ceased in the everlasting summer day was becoming an annoyance to Joergen. He saw the birds sitting on the branches singing, but one by one they would keel over and fall exhausted to the ground, their tired refrain trailing behind them. He felt bound to pick them up and carry them to their sleeping quarters. Next morning their renewed twittering and jumping around him, as he was watering his mother's garden, filled him with tedium.

"Your brow is pale," my son, "your heart is not warm," his mother said one day, "a trip South might do you good."

Even the silvery tinkling song of the skylark, more exquisite than the flute, was irritating him and sounded falsetto.

"I'll go South, mother, but not too far South, where the sun might hit me directly overhead," he told her, 'and maybe even pierce the organ that is my heart,' he thought to himself. He was a cool fellow and knew where his welfare lay.

One morning he breakfasted on gruel to lubricate his joints for the journey, and set out toward sunrays that would touch him at an angle more acute than obtuse.

Staying on sunlit paths and well out of the shadow of the woods, Joergen began to warm up. The pale-green of his brow receded to the roots of his hair and down to his toes, giving way to a rosy hue. He cheerfully stepped over one latitude after another, and since he was a tall fellow, he did not need to raise his feet too high.

Somewhere along latitude forty-two he began to feel just right, and he decided to go no farther South.

One day, Joergen, the lanky, stretched out youth, met Jubo who was short and squat. The actual day was truly forgotten, but not the consequences.

Jubo always carried a pick-axe over his hunched shoulders. He was well-meaning but ignorant, except in the ways of the earth. He lived close to its undulations and was familiar with what were secrets to others, hidden under its surface. He knew them because of what came through the crevices, some of which he had made himself with his pick-axe. He knew of the slithering movement of the earthworm, and with a slow gaze he would follow its drill-like motion into the ground. He knew of the scurrying ways of the chipmunk as it darted between the rocks. He would follow it with his quick, black eyes until his ear could no longer hear its sharp chirping.

Jubo spent his youth eradicating dandelions. He lived in a land where they had become a ubiquitous and pestiferous weed. He did not know these words, but if he did, he could not have expressed it more strongly. He found out that the plant's root could pierce the ground as much as a foot deep, straight down, and that his using his pick-axe was the only sure way of getting rid of the weed.

In the course of his work Jubo developed mixed feelings toward the dandelion: he hated it and loved it, and he held it in awe. He hated its strength and pervasiveness; he loved its beauty when he saw little children blow on the light pappus of delicate white hairs and watch the fruit float off in the air on the waves of their wishes. He had heard of the Russian dandelion, with its root half an inch in diameter and, in Russia, a commercial source of rubber.

That, and its name Kok-saghyz, filled Jubo with awe.

But, as duty called, and putting his feelings aside, Jubo would heave his pick-axe high over his head and let it come down into the ground near the dandelion with a force that reverberated through the entire meadow. With the soil so loosened he would hold the plant by its dentate leaves and triumphantly pull it out. He had only known such pleasure at other times, when he would seize a mop of hair of the woman he had loved and hated, and hear her scream and beg him to let go.

That particular day Joergen was pacing East and West along his chosen latitude. He met Jubo in a field of dandelions.

"Hail," said Joergen, "what a wonderful field of salad and potherbs."

"It's all a weed," Jubo replied.

"What do you mean 'a weed'?"

"A weed is an unwanted plant, in my way of thinking."

"An unwanted plant?" repeated Joergen, experiencing for the first time on his journey and far away from his motherland a touch of warmth in the region of his belly.

He remembered the taste, though slightly bitter, of a salad that his mother used to make, and the wafting aroma as she stirred a hot brew of dandelion leaves.

She was a nature-conscious woman who taught him respect for the milkweed and for any other plant that yields milk as its juice. She was also an educated woman.

"The dandelion," she once told him, "bears its name from dent-de-lion, French for lion's tooth… not to be confused, my son," she added glancing just above his mid-riff where his cool heart lay, "with Coeur de Lion, the name of a brave and warm-hearted English king."

Joergen looked at the tooth-like lobes of the dandelion leaves and remembered his mother's words.

"Yes, an unwanted plant," Jubo said again, as he lifted his pick-axe in the usual manner to show Joergen his skill at removing it.

As Joergen made a move to stop Jubo, the angle of the pick-axe shifted, and instead of falling next to it, the point of the pick pierced the center of the plant. The two men stood stunned and silent as they watched the dandelion, bleeding.

'Not to be confused, my son, with Coeur de Lion…' Joergen heard his mother's words as the warmth from his belly shifted to the organ that was his heart.

Just then he heard the song of the skylark high above the meadow, and he knew that it was the most beautiful song he had ever heard.

He was ready to return home.

Our Gentleman

There was a gentleman in Chattanooga who loved cats. He had one waiting for him at home while he sat at a bar driven there by his transgressions. With his arms akimbo, he occasionally raised them to sip his beer chased with whisky. The dirt under his fingernails and the dust in the wrinkles on his dried up and cracked leather shoes betrayed a lack of gentlemanly care. Yet, in his checkered pants frayed at the cuffs, the elbows of his shirt held fast by leather patches, he could have been, but for his derelict state a Knut Hamsun, or a Hemingway, or a Paul Bowles on one of his rare trips from Morocco by way of USA to his native England. Or, for that matter, an Ian Fleming, pondering on his next "Mr. Bond." Having heard of the Two Gentlemen of Verona, he first tried to model himself on one of them, but he didn't have either a Julia or a Sylvia. Neither did he know if he was one of the gentlemen who preferred blondes. So he decided to just be himself.

None of this would have mattered because, right now, all our gentleman could think of was his cat and the lyrics Chattanooga-choo-choo. And even that song with all its wails and wheels drove the train of his thoughts to nowhere.

He had once been a member of a circus, "Barnum and Bailey" no less, when it wound through narrow streets of a seaport on the Atlantic. So puffed up was the circus that it almost pushed the whole street a few yards into the sea.

In the meantime, our gentleman's mother sat and waited for him in the distant Arkansas. He did not return.

"I love you, ma, but great things await me," he wrote in his final note in response to his mother's crying and fussing.

Great things yes, but he didn't know which ones. Would it be on the circus trampoline, or swallowing fire, or be cut in two by a magician's trick? He tried them all, but it was the expanses of

America, the land that was his land and it was sounding a clarion call. He said good-bye to his companions, the co-jumpers, the co-fire-swallowers, and co-bodies cut in two.

The clarion call led him through low and high roads first to a valley of the dead, better known as the Death Valley. Our gentleman thought hard before he drove into the valley because it was too soon for him to be one of the dead. He backed out his jalopy, and soon found a motel ran by an Indian couple, as such establishments often had been. But the charge was too high and they did not accept the cat, which he had picked up a while ago on one of the roads he had traveled. He moved on.

Actually, it had not been on a road but in a small animal shelter that he acquired the cat. It was in a chintzy town on a vast desert plain of scrubby vegetation and low-lying cacti and mountains in the distance, one of those towns that pepper so much of America and, contrary to all that had been said and written, that give the countryside a particular character and charm. That's where the thought to acquire a cat had struck him. The town consisted of one-story houses along a main street that housed all you'd ever need—a drugstore that sold everything besides drugs, a diner that had the best meat loaf cooked by the owner's wife who, on the side, sold paraphernalia of all kinds like necklaces she had made from old glass beads, which over the years she had picked up in junk shops, also mittens, and scarves she had knitted with wool from a couple of her torn sweaters; there were mugs, some with a chip on the rim that nobody would notice.

There was no US Post Office, but on a street parallel to the main there was a one-room schoolhouse for the town's brightest kids. The others stayed home by mom's skirt or, having advanced to teen age, played pool in the local drinking hole. Only soda for them, but their older brothers would sometimes sneak in something more worth drinking.

There was a dump on the outskirts, and at the opposite end a luxury motel, so labeled on a high poster just outside town to catch the occasional passenger's attention. Our gentleman was caught by such. He spent a night there chasing cockroaches, but a better game yet awaited him. Through a torn window screen an opossum tried to make its way inside. This is what led our gentleman to the animal shelter in search of a cat. Before he purchased one for a few dollars, he asked the shelter's keeper:

"Do you have one on a leash, because I want it for traveling with me?"

"Ah, yes," the man beamed. "A lady passed here recently, and she had a cat on a leash. She had to give up the cat because she was on her way to catch a train in Chattanooga, and they don't take cats on trains there.

"She said it with tears in her eyes, and left her pussy here," the man said.

"So show me the cat," our gentleman said.

Curled up in a cage, a collar round his neck, was a distant descendent of a Bengal tiger—orange with black stripes down its sides. Over the millennia the colors had faded and its ferocity diminished.

"Can I have him for just one night to try him out?" Our gentleman asked.

"That will be two bucks extra."

"OK."

That night our gentleman was awoken by metal cracking, snapping, squeaks and howls, then silence. He grabbed and lit his flashlight, but the cat was nowhere inside the cabin.

Early at dawn he looked out the window and saw the cat in the distance, slowly approaching our gentleman's cabin. He figured the animal passed its test, chasing away an opossum and was returning victorious.

He brought the cat back to the shelter and asked the owner for the leash.

"Oh, the lady took it, said she could use it for a belt."

"A cat with only a collar is no good for me."

"You might find one at the drugstore, but don't think I'll drop the price on the cat."

We next met our gentleman, the cat on the leash, stopping at rest areas, leading the cat to a distant spot to let him pee, to feed him Purina chow and drink water from the emptied can.

Yet something was niggling our gentleman in his relationship with the cat. He was now back, close to Chattanooga, to rejoin his image of a Hamsun, a Hemingway or a Fleming. He felt he should first slow down on its outskirts and consider his transgressions. After making a stop at a motel and settling the cat in the cabin, he unclasped the leash from his collar and twirled it around his own neck. All the leashes and cages that had been used in the service of man loomed before his eyes and weighed so heavily upon him that he had to sit down. Now the leash felt tighter round his neck and tears came to our gentleman's eyes. He didn't know what to do with the cat, release it from the collar, throw away the leash, then what?

This would have been the day to put pen to paper, but nothing would happen. Cats all over the country sat by the fire and ruminated on days gone by whether they've been forgiven their transgressions; none of his own would come to mind.

Minutes passed. The cat hopped on our gentleman's lap, began to purr and licked his hand.

On re-entering Chattanooga, our gentleman took his place at the bar for the day. The next day he was not seen anywhere, or in days thereafter.

Some recounted they saw a puff of smoke from his jalopy down the dirt service road along the railroad tracks. They hoped he had taken his cat with him and not left it to die without food, or water, or out of sadness, missing this our gentleman from Chattanooga.

Unthinkable but Sinkable

The world was in turmoil and lies were circling around the world. His cottage was on a hillside, safe and secure, but in recent days he didn't see any deer in his backyard. They must have moved uphill. He then noticed a small bulge in the green swath of this yard. For a while he didn't give it a thought. But when it became wet, then opened up a bit, and the water began to flow and fill his cellar, he had to give it some thought and went up to the ground floor, which remained dry. The water then lifted the cottage, which began to float downhill to meet the tsunami, almost a thousand feet high from the oncoming ocean below. His cottage was old and fitted all through with wooden pegs; it remained intact.

A stray fox from the woods from beyond his yard, a couple of turkeys that are not given to flight quickly scuttled to the cottage and settled down next to him.

'Am I a modern-day Noah, or an owl or a pussy-cat on a pea-green boat?' he wondered.

The curved lip of land that had marked the horizon was no longer there.

'How long,' he tried to recollect, 'can one survive without food?' Twenty-one days.

'How long without water?' Three to seven days.

He had time. Time for what? To miss his dearly beloved who was to visit him this day? Where was she now? He worried. In the arms of a casual passer-by who tried to keep her afloat? Or trying to rescue her cat that had kept her warm most nights, except when she was at his cottage?

But then he noticed something dropping from above him. Not drops of rain, for the sky was clear.

These were lies. One by one, their weight began to submerge him, and pull the boat and the lies to the bottom of the sea. Until, until, until there were none.

The world was saved, and all that was needed was a man named Noah, in a pea-green boat.

Don't Play the Bassoon

For one indelible moment all lights went out and all sounds ceased to exist.

"Where are the bassoons?" Phil asked his neighbor, the second violin during a brief break. He too was stunned. Phil searched his memory for the time when a strange thing had happened to him before. That experience did not convey the magnitude of the present moment. On that previous occasion Melissa lay naked and curled up in bed and would not speak to him. He tried to cover her with a blanket but she jerked and stopped his attempt.

Then suddenly she asked:

"What did you say?"

That moment had passed and they were now lying comfortably on a beach in Alicante, Spain. He was taking a break from his musical engagement in that dark, soppy London and they were loath to return there. Soppy was nothing unusual, that's how it had always been.

But dark? Yes, dark. Phil remembered another time when all lights in the streets had been turned off at night, traffic was at a minimum, especially after an air raid siren began to wail on and on and on. Then it would stop. Everyone waited for the second wail that would be one continuous sound. They could then return from the Underground Metro, which served as an air raid shelter. Phil and Melissa had managed to get away to Alicante, their first time there, and its beach. They would rise from the sand, frolic in the Mediterranean waters, which had not been targeted for bombing. Fish were exempted from the kill.

That was a couple of years ago, and they were again in Alicante, their favorite place. When they returned from the beach to their hotel and, after a shower, Melissa took up her book to read. He noticed that rather than turning the pages she stared at the bookmark.

"It's supposed to be an abstract, but the painter's inscription says 'John Sage's Subway Madonna,'" she remarked.

"I don't even see that. To me it looks like a twirl of small intestines, then becoming the large bowel," was Phip's reaction. And they talked and discussed and missed their flight to London—anything, it seemed, to delay their return home.

But where were we—ah, the bassoons. Phip hadn't told Melissa that they had been missing. It was actually the people playing them who had been missing. Had they been called for an interrogation, he assumed. And why the bassoons? Could Phip, a first violin be the next one, or his neighbor above, the viola? Could the drums be the next because of their loud booming sound? These heavy sounds seemed to have been the present Supreme Leader's, which he preferred. Those who were close to him saw him cringe at high tones of clarinets.

Times were uneasy for Phip and Melissa. The Supreme Leader had issued an edict that certain "elements" were unnecessary or dangerous to his regime. His subordinates obeyed and total darkness was necessary to carry out his mission, usually in groups. The trouble was that there might be someone in a group who'd rather abstain.

Phip happened to know one such person, his friend, a flautist. His name was Judd.

"So far I haven't said or objected to anything," he told Phip.

"But can't they notice by your attitude?" Phip asked.

"Not so far, but it's all a matter of time."

"What happens to those who do?"

"Our country is large." This seemed like a non-sequitor, but he continued: "There are the wide Yorkshire wilds, where anyone can get lost. Of course there are the high White Cliffs of Dover, or the tall and scraggly coast of the Orkneys…"

"But their bodies would wash ashore…" Phil interrupted.

"They're tied to weights, and the waters are deep…" He was

going to continue, but he suddenly stopped and gave his friend a shush sign. They were sitting on a bench in a park, and Judd noticed a strange object stuck in between two branches of a tree not far from them.

"Our Supreme Leader is great, a quiet man, I'm told..." Judd made a sudden change to a raised voice, "but he deserves it and needs to be celebrated."

"How?"

"That depends on his mood," Judd said, "it could be a procession on Regent Street, the bassoons blaring, or on Oxford Street, the drums booming."

"So?"

"He's not really musical, but these sounds seem to suit him."

"I'm glad I'm not playing either of them, or I'd be the next one to go." Phip remarked under his breath.

That being said they quickly left, each in his own direction. When Phil reached home he saw a note on the table.

"I'll be back at noon, Melissa."

She wasn't there at noon or the next day, and Phip was worried about her. He and Judd shouldn't have chatted under that tree.

Phip didn't see her until two weeks later, the day of the Leader's re-election, when a huge crowd of well-wishers gathered at Piccadilly Circus. He climbed a couple of steps of the Eros statue in the center to have a better view. That's when he saw her in the middle of it and unreachable. She was singing and shouting hoorah to the Leader with the rest of them.

As he was climbing down the steps, in the far distance he could hear a clarinet playing a different tune. He rushed home for his violin to join him.

Where Rosehips Grew

Nothing has changed here. Day followed night, night followed day. I liked routine as much as I had ever done. I was not afflicted by any illness, only by life, running on or out. The catastrophe has already happened, so I am writing this post factum. It was not that a child hasn't shown up for the school bus to take him home and years later his bones were found in the neighboring woods. It was not the nuclear explosion in Chernobyl where, besides the human tragedy, fields of strawberries in neighboring countries became radioactive.

If you happened to see a photograph of the Wellesley campus in the AWP "Chronicle," it shows dots of people sitting on a huge lawn, and some distance beyond and above there is a view of trees that look like a huge, menacing cloud. The people on the lawn do not seem to be aware of anything happening. Nor was I, at first, like the people on the lawn, as I was sitting on a beach of a peninsula on the nearby Atlantic coast.

Gradually a hum, then a louder and louder noise scared me. I got up, ran to the shore and dove into the water. I swam to the opposite shore about a couple of miles away—that's how strong I was and the fear that propelled me. I got up, cleared the sand from the in between the toes of my right foot, but forgot about the left.

"Well, hello, Harry, what on earth?!" exclaimed a woman, when she saw me panting and dripping with water.

I looked at her with my water-bleared eyes and finally recognized as someone I had known years ago.

"I thought there was smoke across the bay, from a fire, which the fire brigade had trouble extinguishing, it seemed to last so long. But what on earth?"

When I finally caught my breath, I said I just got scared and swam, and I hobbled toward her, forgetting the sand between toes of my left foot.

The woman, I didn't quite remember her name, Monika I think, had changed considerably. Her auburn red hair of my memory was now a mousy blond, but her eyes were still tinged with green—frequently the color scheme of a seductive female of our species—she was lowering her eyelids as if mocking. But the color scheme is not only of our species. Green-eyed orange tabby cats are similarly colored, and when it, let's say it's a she, lowers her lids she has no mocking intent, as far as we know, it's merely a prelude to sleep.

People were sluggish from heat that summer. Sluggish to notice, or hear or ask, or recognize what was happening, and I had swam not a couple of miles, it seemed, but a whole ocean of distance. Slow was the movement of events, slow were news in arriving and slow was our awareness in receiving them.

Especially Monika and I were not there yet. She offered me her former boyfriend's clothes, and all she did was to suggest where I could stay and that we meet next day to catch up on events of our lives in years intervening to the present.

We were at a café the following day.

Monika didn't seem perturbed by the distant shadow across the bay, slowly growing. Looking at her and furtively squinting through a window in that direction, I was not about to interrupt our conversation. Not even to mention that my house was right there, across the water, though not within the access of the fire, if that's what it was, not yet. I had left only a few belongings, no need to worry about what may or may not happen.

The cause of the gray cloud, that was its color, was not yet reaching my awareness. I had right here enough of a preamble to my own calamity. As Monika had reached out her hand to shake mine when we had come together at the café, she gently moved her thumb across the palm of my hand—perhaps an illusion of mine. In some countries it's a sign of a 'come-on.'

After several such meetings she said I could use a bunk bed at her house, and I moved in with her.

I lay in my bed many at night, how many nights I didn't know. I now realize, many years later, how slowly, at that time, events had slipped through my consciousness. I had even been slow clearing the sand from in between the toes of my left foot. Monika kept me busy with chores in her house and backyard, and kept me in cash.

Time dragged on. No, it was the news that dragged on in coming. I noticed the autumn slowly setting in. A blush of pink began to tinge the magnificent sedum spectabile that covered a large part of her backyard and the brush slowly turning into a fiery color.

But what about the sand that I had not cleared from in between the toes of my left foot? Some vegetation began to show there. I'm sure you've noticed how moss grows on rocks devoid of soil or grasses sprout from arid, sandy soil. To my amazement, a tiny plant had begun to grow between my toes. When I tossed it into the garden it turned into a rosehip bush that usually grows by the seacoast. Monika made jelly out of the rosehips for our breakfast table, my only contribution to our material world.

When the news finally arrived, the jelly that Monika had made no longer tasted sweet, and she became less talkative. Instead of the usual hug in the morning, she just stroked the top of my head and smiled weakly. My heart gave extra bumps, but I took her queue and began to speak as little as she. Our lovemaking became perfunctory.

"What is the matter?" I would ask.

"Oh, nothing."

"Strange that a man would have suddenly beached on my shore," she remarked one morning.

"What?! Beached like bloody whale or a seal, or some other slimy mammal?

I went on with my usual shopping for us, her special tangerines or clementines, etc., etc., she paid no attention.

"I don't seem to feel the same about you," she said sometime into the following month.

"Why? What happened?" I asked.

"I don't know," she said, "you're a fine gentleman, but something's off."

The clouds on the horizon had long been gone, perhaps they had affected her in some way. Bow we seem to have drifted into our own.

"I'm tired of the ocean, the water constantly lapping against the shore."

"So?"

"I'd like to visit my grandmother for a while, she has a cottage in the mountains."

No mention of my coming along. I noticed her swimsuit, a bit old I grant you, thrown into the trash bin. What? Wasn't she coming back here, soon, or not at all?

One day I saw a taxi at the door and she, with a suitcase, came from upstairs.

"What's this? Don't you want me to take you to the bus depot or the train or whatever?!"

"Not this time… you're a fine gentleman, Harry, I'll always cherish that."

The taxi hooted, I helped her with her bag. The last glimpse I had was the taxi rounding the corner of our street.

'Not this time…' kept ringing in my head for days and nights, for months.

I, too, should have moved, but I stayed where I was and felt the sting of every object that we had shared, of the café downtown we both enjoyed, the bumps in the sidewalk she had tripped over. The où sont les neiges d'antant—a horrible cliché by now, clinging to my brain cells, which could not be dislodged.

Then came a letter addressed in Monika's handwriting. Strange, she sensed I had not moved.

"Dear Harry, I think I owe you an explanation." No, I don't need it, I'd rather stay with my chagrin. But I read on. "There are things that topsy-turvy our psyche…" How could she have used such a trite expression? "Sorry, Harry, topsy-turvy doesn't describe it… it was more like poison that I didn't identify right away. It took me months. I sensed it first like a particle of grit in my mouth. We laughed about the sand in between your toes, the rosehips. Then, people began to talk… the peninsula across the water, the granite… the human error… the mayhem that must have ensued. The TV was showing explosions, dismembered bodies. I had bad dreams, couldn't handle it anymore. My emotions turned off, against our lovemaking in particular, I couldn't talk about it. I had to go away…" Then there was some scribbling I couldn't decipher.

Yes, the peninsula… the news had finally arrived. That tract of land consisted mainly of layers of granite. It had been mined for years and transported to many places, including to New York for foundations of its buildings. As a technique of excavation, dynamite rods had been placed in several places. What did this mean, how many places? The powers consulted with each other, but not enough, hardly enough as to the numbers and locations of the rods. Someone pressed a wrong button at city hall.

You Can't Talk This Way

The events of the story to be told here are still fresh in some people's minds because of some odd things that happened in their neighbor's backyard. So is the bitterness with which a student's relationship with his Professor, whom he came to love and admire, had begun.

"You can't talk this way," the Professor had said.

"Why can't I talk this way?" the Student asked.

"Because you don't know enough about these things," the Professor replied.

"Still, why not?"

"Because you're not supposed to," he replied again.

"And not talk this way? Should I sing it or yell?"

"Just get off that proverbial soap box."

"Why should I?"

"Because few people will understand you."

"My friends on the West Coast might."

Thus began their relationship, as they sat one day at a table in a college cafeteria, and it went on until the Professor's approaching demise.

The Student's name was Abe. He had recently graduated from college, majoring in astronomy. Such things as dust in the cosmos had for him a major meaning.

The ailing Professor liked Abe and was generous with his time. In their conversations they didn't ignore the elephant in the room—death, the Professor's approaching death.

"Aren't you afraid of it?" Abe asked him at one of their meetings.

"Afraid?...No, not at all. I could talk about it for hours or days, or even weeks or months, if I had the time," the Professor replied.

"What do you mean?"

"Have you read Beckett?"

"Only his plays."

"Try his novels, and especially Malone Dies."

"I beg your pardon, sir, but I don't think we have the time… Can you help me?"

"He talks about the process of slow death, which in more conventional terms we call life. But he is not humorless about it, as his notes about a Buster Keaton show, Keaton's expressionless face as he encounters torments and suffering."

"So we should face death with humor?"

"Not strictly so, but certainly not with a tragic face."

It was obvious that the Professor was becoming tired, so they postponed more talking for another day.

But something was niggling Abe. There was a missing link between death and what Abe had learned in astronomy—the eventual "death" of all matter as would for example happen in the predicted explosion of our sun, and with it of our earth. So where were we in this? Where would be all the souls, all the bodies to be reincarnated, which various religions are telling us about?

This was the kind of thing he could not talk about with his wife Cathy, a steadfast Catholic.

Talk was one thing, but acting upon his thoughts was another. What was the dust on his desk, when he deeply pondered it?

"Thou art dust and unto dust thou shalt return." Were the Ancients on to something?

The dust he was looking at, right there on his desk, contained both the remnants of organic matter as well as the interplanetary particles, atoms of helium, hydrogen, carbon, oxygen, etc., which had formed the organic matter.

"This is serious business," he thought to himself, and he could not get up the nerve to clear the dust. He just did not dare to do it himself. But perhaps his wife Cathy would help.

"Cathy, would you mind wiping the dust off my desk?" he asked her. She was his faithful companion in domestic chores.

In her mind faithful yes and no, but when she stopped in a

café in town, some people heard her say to her friends how odd this request was: "and he meant it not just once, but all the time from now on."

Coming from a long line of Irish Catholics, when it came to more weighty matters such as life and death, they would often come to blows, not in the manner of the Irish Donnybrook fights but just perfectly civil exchanges.

"So you believe in God," he would say with a smirk.

"Of course I do, what else is there?"

"Science."

"So you believe in Science, do you?" she would retort with a smirk of her own.

"I don't believe in it, it's not a God or religion."

"What is it then?"

"A series of facts derived by observation, by experiments, preferably double-blind."

"But it's often wrong."

"Of course it is, but isn't God often wrong? And please give me some factual examples of his existence."

At this moment Cathy would realize that there was no point in further discussion. Her brothers, Patrick and Shawn, had often warned her not to get involved with this guy Abe.

However, Abe and Cathy almost did come to blows when questions arose about having children. Abe could never tell her, a Catholic, what was in his mind. He had read that Beckett compared the parental instinct to criminal tendency, when you consider life as a continuous series of torments and suffering. Abe wasn't sure what Beckett meant by it, but he thought that religions have a lot do with it. For good or for evil, God's punishment for this and that, burning in hell if you're bad; it just didn't make sense.

In Abe's mind, self-conflagration would be the only act that would combine the two points of view: turning into dust (ashes, in common parlance) and putting an end to torment and suffering.

He remembered the Professor's dictum that few people would understand him. So he just went on with his life and continued to ask Cathy to wipe off the dust.

However, Abe was not the kind of man who would leave things alone. He often visited the Professor and they would have lively discussions. This took up Abe's time, and Cathy began to wonder what was going on, was he "seeing" someone?

She was too shy to ask him directly, but it occurred to her that a ruse might work: she stopped wiping the dust from Abe's desk.

At first he did not notice it. A pile of dust does not make much of a pile. But a desk is not much of a desk unless it serves a purpose—for carrying books, scraps of Abe's writings and so on. So dust began to settle on these things, and it began to fill a glass container for his pens and pencils. It was this that finally caught his attention because the glass began to look murky and his pens smudged his notes.

"Cathy, what's the matter? Aren't you dusting my things anymore?"

Shy as she was, Cathy blushed.

"I'm too busy these days," she replied.

"Too busy with what?"

She felt caught and couldn't answer. Now things turned around to her being the culprit.

"With this and that, errands downtown and so forth."

Abe was a placid fellow, but now he felt ire rising.

"What is this 'so forth,' are you "seeing" someone?"

"No, I'm not."

"Must be something pretty serious for you to neglect our deal about your wiping off the dust!"

He rose from his chair and left the room, then the house with a bang, a sign of his torment and suffering. The bang was so loud that some people, especially the neighbors couldn't help overhearing it.

Cathy was uneasy about how things were turning out between them. But she remembered how well she had got along in college with her professor of physics, how easy it was to talk to him. She found his address and phone in the college directory and called him up. He was happy to see her.

The professor, now retired, lived off campus. He welcomed her into his dingy apartment with its faint aroma of decay.

"Sorry, Cathy, this place hasn't been cleaned in a while, in this half-life existence of mine."

"What do you mean?"

"You may remember from my teaching you in class about how radioactive substances decay in half-life?"

"What on earth do you mean? You're not radioactive."

"Well, I'm using this as a metaphor, and I consider life as being such a substance."

"But professor, sir, you are not decaying!"

Cathy sounded horrified and disgusted.

"I'm more than half-life there."

"You are not ill, are you, professor?"

"Yes I am."

"Oh dear, aren't you afraid of what's finally going to happen?"

The professor was getting a bit tired, Cathy noticed.

"Can I fix you a cup of tea or coffee?"

"That would be lovely. I still have all the ingredients in my kitchenette."

The first sip of hot tea restored him. However, he sensed that in their conversation they were beginning to tread on dangerous ground. He had an eerie feeling that he was dealing with something familiar. But Cathy boomed right into it.

"Do you believe in God?"

"Why do you ask? Have you been talking about this with someone?"

"Yes, my husband. It worries me the way he talks about it."

"What's his name?"

"Abe."

"Oh dear. I had someone by that name in my class, a few years before you."

"Do you ever see him?"

"Yes, he comes here quite a lot and we talk about such things."

"But that's my husband!"

"Say hello to him from me when you get home."

"You've no idea how relieved I am!"

"So do you share some of these ideas?"

Here Cathy did not feel inclined to share why she really came to see the professor, about her marital concerns.

"You seem tired, professor, perhaps we can talk about this some other time. You've been so kind to let me visit you."

"Yes, my child, some other time…" He drifted off into a snooze.

Cathy put a blanket over him as he was reclining on an armchair, and slowly, quietly left.

The crisis being over between them, Cathy decided to take a trip somewhere. Abe was too busy with his work, so she made arrangements to go alone. She had always wanted to go to Chesapeake Bay and stay in one of the hotels there. She found one overlooking the ocean, with an easy downhill access to the beach, and she booked herself there for a couple of weeks, off season, so it didn't cost much.

It had room service, so she breakfasted in bed. Eggs over easy, buttered toast, raspberry jam served in a small crystal bowl and great coffee in a ceramic pot. The plates were so beautiful that she turned one over to look at the make. It said Limoges. It didn't mean anything to her, but she loved them.

Meanwhile, since the Professor wasn't clear why Cathy had come to see him, next time he saw Abe he thought better not to mention it and focus their conversation on what was of more interest to them.

"What do you think about the soul?" he asked Abe.

"I don't have one."

"What!?'"

"As I said, I don't have one."

"You are the first person I ever heard say such a thing."

"Well, here you have it."

"That's what I meant when I told you that you can't talk this way."

"It's not just talk."

"What do you mean?"

"I'm not sure yet, but some time you'll hear about it."

"So what do you have instead of it, if anything?"

"Consciousness."

"What about matters of good and evil?"

"Oh, I do have a conscience, and it's all in my mind which is lodged in the brain."

"You talk like a stalwart physicist."

"I have to think of something concrete before Cathy comes home from her trip, because I have trouble listening to all that religious talk from her."

He went to their backyard. A pile of dirt and something burnt in it would do the trick, he thought. A smell wafting into the neighbors' yard would certainly cause concern.

About a week went by, Cathy had notes from Abe delivered to her on a tray by one of the hotel's staff. But then the notes stopped coming and she got worried. Perhaps he was off to a conference somewhere, she wondered. Anyway she decided to cut her trip a couple of days short and sent Abe a note about it.

When she arrived at the airport his car wasn't there, so she had to take a taxi home. She then saw a brief note on a side table in the hall: "Go to the backyard. I love you, Cathy, Abe."

When she went to the backyard she saw a small pile of dirt piled up, like a foot square. As she came closer she noticed a note next to it on the ground held down by a couple of rocks. She picked it up and began to read:

"Cathy dearest,

"We've had good times, but there is between us a huge rift of understanding. I've decided to show you what I mean in a more drastic and concrete way. You'll see it when you look at the pile of dirt. From now on call it dust, ashes, whatever you like, ponder its meaning and revise your views or not.

"I've often thought but didn't tell you that self-conflagration would be the only act that would combine my two points of view: turning into dust (ashes, in common parlance) and putting an end to torment and suffering. I don't know about the "self" part of it, but conflagration is what the funeral homes do all the time.

"As you look at that pile think of it as all that's left of me. Do you see anything like a soul hovering around it? Have a good look and come to your own conclusions."

"Love,

Abe"

Cathy was flabbergasted, and bent down to look at the pile closer. A smell reached her nostrils as if something had been burnt. Now terrified and in no mood to look for Abe's soul, she ran back to the house and flopped down in an armchair to recover her breath. Only then did she think to check the garage. Abe's car was there and this scared her even more—was he really in that pile? How could it be? Self- conflagration???! This would explain the lack of his notes to me when I was still in Chesapeake Bay, ran through her head.

Minutes passed, she couldn't move. She then heard a faint noise coming from upstairs, like a suppressed cough, or a chuckle. She ran into their bedroom, where Abe was reclining on an armchair.

"What on earth is this?" she exclaimed.

"Self-conflagration… I certainly thought of it, but couldn't go through with it. I hope I made a point though."

"You idiot!"

She ran down the stairs and out the door with a bang that the neighbors must have heard.

The bang still rang in Sophie's ears, as she was weeding in her front yard when Cathy, her friend, arrived.

"Who does he think he is?"

"What do you mean? Who?"

"Didn't you smell something in my back yard a few days ago, when I was still away?"

"Well yes, I thought Abe was fixing a barbeque."

"A barbeque, my foot!"

"I wish he'd barbequed himself!"

"Oh, Cathy, what on earth…?"

"I don't know, that job of his must have gone to his head."

From one word to another, many cups of tea over time, Cathy tried to convey to Sophie, "as friend to friend," the lack of "understanding" between her and Abe, which he had tried to covey.

"And no children either!" she once blurted out in the middle of her harangues.

"Ooooh?!"

"No. Didn't you notice?"

"Well, I must say… not one of my business, close as we are. How long have you two been married? Time must have flown since the wedding we all attended."

"A couple of years."

Sophie's shocked reaction was a surprise. Was she, the wife, the "idiot" in her love-making with Abe? Which one of them was avoiding contraception? She certainly was not. Was either one of them sterile? Someone wasn't paying attention, it suddenly dawned on her.

"Perhaps if we try to bring him closer to God?" Sophie suggested.

"Not a fat chance."

"Doesn't he believe in God?"

"No."

"Then how does he think we, everything was created?"

"By something like a big bang, then hydrogen and helium."

"Oh, boy. You are in big trouble."

The same day, at supper, Cathy told Abe that she'd like to go and visit her parents in Wichita, Kansas for a while.

"Why? You're always going visiting somewhere."

"It's my parents, I need to see them. But we'll be in touch." Small help to him, he felt.

She realized her visit would be awkward, their hankering to be grandparents, and they would be of no help in settling her mind to have no children. But she went anyway.

For a while they exchanged notes as usual.

But, as usual, after a couple of weeks his notes stopped coming. What is it now, Cathy wondered.

"I should have talked to him first," she thought. But she knew she'd be grasping at straws, and sink into a hole anyway.

Yet returning home sooner than planned seemed a necessity, just as she was contemplating getting a ride on an air balloon. Those balloons are so beautiful, you can see a vast country from inside them. Wichita, a cow town in the olden days, now "The air capital of the world," famous for its manufacturing of various types of aircraft—Cathy was thinking about it all, as she was reluctantly arranging her trip home.

When she arrived at the airport Abe's car wasn't there, so again there had to be a taxi ride home. His car was in the garage. She then saw a brief note on a side table in the hall.

"Oh dear, another note," she sighed:

"Go to the backyard. I love you, Cathy, Abe."

Only then did she realize that someone next door, was it Sophie, went through Cathy's mind, had peeked through a door and didn't say anything like 'oh, hello Cathy, how was your trip?' or another one on the opposite side, who had just come back from shopping with groceries, turned away when she saw Cathy coming.

She went to the backyard where she had so tenderly planted a row of pink azaleas that would bloom later in the spring and where rows of white crocuses were already opening up, the spring was so beautiful this year, but those in the front were somewhat singed.

A yellow police tape was surrounding an area in the center

of the yard, where some dirt was piled up. There was a note next to it, somewhat singed but still legible, which Cathy read: "On no account is this pile to be examined or cleared and the yellow tapes removed by the police until the return of the owner of the house." As she looked around she saw an undamaged note pinned on the fence. She tore it off and began to read it:

"Cathy dearest,

"We've had good times, but there is between us a huge rift of understanding, which I can no longer tolerate.

"I had good intentions, though. As a recompense for no child, I thought of getting you a lama from a farm up north in Maine, or a cat from our local animal shelter. But the lama might spit in your face and the cat might scratch your hand. So I gave up the idea.

"I've wanted to show you again what I mean about the world I want to live in. Here is my more drastic and concrete expression of what I mean. You'll see it when you look at the pile of dirt. Call it dust, ashes, whatever you like, ponder its meaning and revise your views or not, but I will no longer be part of it.

"I've often thought but didn't tell you that self-conflagration would be the only act that would combine my two points of view: turning into dust (ashes, in common parlance) and putting an end to torment and suffering. I don't know about the "self" part, I'll decide on it at the last minute.

"This time have a really good look at the pile and think of it as all that's left of me. And I urge you again: do you see anything like a soul hovering around it?

"I realize that after this you may not want to see me in what you consider "the hereafter," but rest assured that I'm leaving you with no ill will, but with all my love instead. May this sustain you in all your torment and suffering, for ever and ever, amen, Abe."

By this time Cathy was all in tears and wailing so loudly that her neighbors could hear her and came over to comfort her.

"Wha... wha... wha... happe...?" She could hardly blurt out her question.

"We're so sorry, so sorry, Cathy."

"Be sure our hearts are with you."

"But what happen… wha… happened?"

"At first we smelled an awful stench…"

"We thought Abe was burning some stinking clothes, then something meat-like that didn't smell right."

"We were getting suspicious."

"For a while we thought nothing of it, perhaps Abe was preparing a barbeque."

"But then there was this awful ball of fire, and we immediately called the police. Put our hoses to it."

They had all been talking over each other.

"By the time they arrived, they took their time, told us they had another terrible emergency along the way, there was this smoldering pile and a note still on the fence, the note that you've just read."

"The police went into the garage and told us that Abe's car was still there."

Cathy, numb in her shock, called the police and, giving them a description of Abe's shirt that she had found missing earlier among his clothes, she asked them for a search. DNA testing of the ashes was inconclusive.

After a while of fruitless search Cathy put the house on sale and moved away to live with her friends in Oshkosh, Wisconsin.

The search still continued anywhere anyone could think of, in the Midwest, up and down the coasts, especially on the Pacific Coast, which Abe had hinted about to the Professor, and brought no results.

A cold case remains to this day.

Epilogue

I am a Polish-born retired psychiatrist, now a writer of short stories. Many years ago, and close to my retirement from my clinical practice and from my position as Clinical Instructor in Psychiatry at the Harvard Medical School, something extraordinary happened—a latent desire for literary creativity suddenly emerged. In my search for publication of a few of my stories I came across Andrei Codrescu's "The Exquisite Corpse—a Journal of Ideas." The partly surreal style of my writing caught Codrescu's interest, and he went on to publish all my stories until the magazine's demise in the late 1990s.

I do not classify myself as a surrealist writer, but I often use a surreal way to express something real. I had attended writers' workshops for many summers at Skidmore College—most helpful to me as a writer in an acquired but my much-admired English language. The best description of my work was provided me by the author Russell Banks, as one of my instructors at Skidmore College: "your writing is on the borderline of Polish and South American Surrealism but it is grounded on the American soil," the soil that I had traveled far and wide; to other parts of the world as well, each place an inspiration for a story.

Had I not practiced writing literary though somewhat idiosyncratic English I would not have been able to become an award-winning translator of Witold Gombrowicz's equally idiosyncratic Polish prose in his four novels.

I humbly present this reflection as an only child of the first Polish aviatrix who taught me how to knit and crochet and a sea captain who told me "don't darn socks (as was the custom in those days—D.B.), read books instead."

~D.B.

Biography

Danuta Borchardt is a Polish-born émigré, living in the United States since 1959. She is a retired psychiatrist and retired Instructor of Clinical Psychiatry at the Harvard Medical School. Now a writer of short stories, some surrealist and influenced by André Breton's Surrealist Movement in the 1920s, which were published in the "Exquisite Corpse" in the 1980s 1990s.

Borchardt has traveled extensively through the backlands and other parts of the United States. A stranger to this land, she found these places exotic, and they provided inspiration for many of her stories. She has earned Russell Banks' opinion that her writing is "on the borderland of Polish and South American surrealism yet grounded on the American soil."

She is an awarded translator of Polish Literature, and in 2018 she was a participant in a translation of the scholarly writings by Janusz Korczak (1878-1942) a Polish educator, martyred by the Germans; all above are into English.

She is best known for having brought to Anglophone readers four novels by the internationally acclaimed Polish exile writer Witold Gombrowicz (1904-1969): *Ferdydurke* (Yale, 2000, *Cosmos* (Yale, 2005), *Pornografia* (Grove, 2009), and *Trans-Atlantyk* (Yale 2014). Borchardt's translations of Gombrowicz's novels have enjoyed tremendous critical success. She has been awarded the National Translation Award, a fellowship by the National Endowment for the Arts and the Found in Translation Award.

Other Titles by Textshop Editions

Defense Mechanism by Krzysztof Siwczyk
Sonnet 100 by Marilyn Allen
Library Of— by Dan Beachy-Quick

www.ingramcontent.com/pod-product-compliance
Lightning Source LLC
Chambersburg PA
CBHW070047260626
47159CB00005B/2139